The Hunchback of Notre Dame

by Victor Hugo

ADAPTED BY ROBIN MOORE

ALADDIN PAPERBACKS

Adaptation copyright © 1996 by Robin Moore. Adapted from *The Hunchback of Notre Dame* by Victor Hugo, first published in 1831.

Aladdin Paperbacks
An imprint of Simon & Schuster
Children's Publishing Division
1230 Avenue of the Americas
New York, NY 10020

First Aladdin Paperbacks Edition, June 1996

Printed and bound in the United States of America

10 9 8 7 6 5 4 3 2 1

Library of Congress Catalog Card Number: 96-84440

ISBN 0-689-81027-X

❧ Contents ❧

❧ Pronunciation Guide ❧

(The syllables in capital letters are stressed.)

Clopin Trouillefuo: klo-PAN tru-ee-FO

de Greve: di GREV

Dom Claude Frollo: DOM KLAWD FRO-yo

Florian: flor-ee-ON

Gudule: goo-DOOL

Guernsey: gern-ZEE

Jacques Charmolue: ZHAK shar-mo-LOO

Notre Dame: NO-tr DAM

Phoebus: FEE-bus

Pierrat Torterue: peer-AH tor-te-RUE

Pierre Gringoire: pee-AIR gran-GWAR

Quasimodo: kwa-zee-MO-doe

Rheims: RAMZ

Seine: SEN

❧ Introduction ❧

I KNOW I AM UGLY TO LOOK UPON.

My face is so horrible that pregnant women will not even turn their gaze in my direction, for fear their babies will be born as ugly as I.

I am so hideous that children run in fear from me, clutching their mothers' skirts.

Even strong men, pretending to be brave, ride by me with their backs held straight. But inside, I know they tremble with fear and revulsion.

I know that I was made by a great craftsman. But I have often wondered: Why did he make me so vile and repulsive? All of Paris turns from my ugliness.

From my perch here on the highest walls of the cathedral of Notre Dame, I can see out over the sloping rooftops and the smoking chimneys of Paris. Down there, in the great square before the church, there is nothing I do not notice. There is no shout or moan, no whispered word or quiet footstep that does not reach my pointed ears. There is no sight that does not pass before my unblinking eyes. And there is no smell, vile or pleasant, that does not drift up into my flaring nostrils. I am always awake, always listening and watching.

The craftsman who made me called me a gargoyle. The laborers who cemented me to this wall called me a demon. The people in the streets below call me insulting names. To them I am only a stone statue, with a horrible face and twisted body, designed to protect the church against intruders.

But in the hundreds of years that I have hung above the city, I have come to understand my true purpose: I know now that I have been placed here to remember all that I have seen, and to tell the secret stories of our town.

The tales of what I do not see directly are brought to me by my friends, the sewer rats of Paris, who can creep into every nook and cranny of the city; and by my other winged friends, the pigeons, who fly over the winding streets and the wide boulevards of the city and come to roost near me in the bell towers of Notre Dame.

You may be asking yourself how a stone can tell a story. It is a good question, one for which I have a ready answer: I have learned that every stone, even the humblest cobblestone in the narrowest, dirtiest street of Paris, has a story to tell. We stones never sleep and have a very long memory. And we willingly tell our stories to anyone who will listen to what we have to say.

But people are strange: they move about quickly, they talk among themselves. Many of them do not listen very well. I hope you will listen. I hope you will open your ears to my words.

Of the many stories I could tell you now, there is

one that stands above all the rest, a tale more heart-breaking and beautiful than anything else the streets of Paris have to offer.

The story I wish to tell you is about a person even uglier than I. This is the story of Quasimodo, the hunchback of Notre Dame, as only I can tell it. . . .

CHAPTER ONE

❧ Companions ❧

I WAS THE ONE WHO SAW QUASIMODO BROUGHT
to our church when he was a young boy. No one saw
what I saw. No one was awake but my brother gargoyles and I, staring down at the darkened streets of
the city. It was late in the fall of 1467.

In the secret hours before dawn, I saw a heavyset,
ragged woman step from the shadows and walk out
into the great square before our church. It was an
October night, cold and clear. The moonlight was
bright and I could see very well.

In her arms, she carried what looked to be a bundle of rags lashed to a wooden board. I watched as she
quietly laid the bundle on the steps. Then she turned
and, without looking back, walked quickly away.

A moment later, I heard something, like the cry of
a wild animal. But as I listened more closely, the
sounds that drifted up to my ears became almost
human. I understood then that the bundle she had
placed on the cold stone steps was not a mass of rags,
it was a living child.

I had seen this happen many times before.

There is a tradition in our church that any
unwanted child can be left on the doorstep of Notre

4

Dame early on a Sunday morning. A person who wishes to adopt one can do so, assured that he or she has done a good deed.

On this Sunday, no one heard the young child cry out, no one but I. It thrashed and cried, lashed to its cradleboard, until it was exhausted, then it fell back to sleep. In the first light of dawn, a group of old women noticed the frost-covered bundle and clustered around it.

"A foundling," I heard one of the old ones say.

"Sleeping well," said another.

"Let us have a look," said a third, bending over the bundle.

But when she folded back the stained handkerchief that covered the child's face, the woman sprang back as if she had been burned by a hot iron.

The howl of the wakened babe filled the cold corners of the square.

The old women covered their heads and scurried away.

I could see now why they had rushed away so quickly.

This child was like none other who had been left on our doorstep. He was a husky boy, three or four years old, but he was horribly deformed. His head was sunk down between his shoulders. His backbone was curved and an ugly hump rose from behind his neck, like a misplaced shoulder. His breastbone protruded and his legs were spindly and twisted.

His head was covered with a tangled and thatchy

forest of red hair. His right eye swam, milky white, behind a half-closed eyelid, while the left one bulged from its socket. His nose was squashed flat, as if the boy had been dropped, facedown, onto a hard stone floor. His mouth was twisted and fouled with spit. Yellowed teeth jutted from his lips like jagged tusks. Over his left eye was an ugly, blackened wart.

You would think no one would dare to adopt such a devilish-looking child. But you would be wrong.

A young priest, Claude Frollo, heard the cry. To everyone's astonishment, Frollo bent and lifted the boy, carrying him up the steps and into the very chambers of our church. From that day forward, Notre Dame became the boy's home. He came to be known as Quasimodo, which means "almost human."

I will never know for sure why Frollo adopted the boy. Some people say it was because he wanted favor with God. Some say it was because the priest's younger brother had recently died. But I think something different.

I knew that Frollo was not what he appeared to be.

In the day, he was a red-robed priest, conducting Mass for the people of Paris or praying piously in the cathedral. But the rats had told me that at night, deep in the cellars of Notre Dame, he practiced the art of sorcery, reading from a strange, leather-bound book and whispering dark words before a blackened candle. I knew then that Frollo's soul was as twisted and tortured as Quasimodo's body. I often wondered if he saw the hunchback as some link to the darker powers of the universe.

I cannot prove this. From all outward appearances, Frollo treated the boy well, if a little sternly.

When Quasimodo was ten years old, Frollo brought him up to the bell towers for the first time and showed him how to ring the great bells. There were fifteen bells all together, fourteen bronze bells with copper tongues and one made from wood. There were fifteen bells—fifteen voices—that spoke to the young boy in a way that no human could. When he set the bells to swinging, a deep and soulful sound filled the air, reverberating through every stone in the church.

In a short time, Quasimodo became the bell ringer of Notre Dame and would faithfully climb to the tower each day to ring the faithful to Mass. But he rang too well. Soon, the great clanging of the bells burst his eardrums and he became deaf to the world.

It was around this time that Quasimodo and I first met.

I think I can safely say that I was Quasimodo's favorite gargoyle. Growing up alone in the church, the deformed boy would often speak to the cold stone statues, perhaps because they were the only ones who would listen to his mangled speech.

But on the day he found me, something special happened. It had stormed the night before—winters in Paris can be cold and gray—and we gargoyles were covered with a thin dusting of snow.

I felt Quasimodo's heavy hands brushing the snow from my head and shoulders. Then, with one bulging and curious eye, he leaned out and looked into my face. It was the meeting of two supremely ugly beings.

You see, in addition to being the gargoyle closest to the bell tower, I am also the ugliest. When the workers were fastening me to these walls, they dropped me, facedown, on the stone floor. A fine crack, so small that no one noticed, appeared on my right cheek. But, as the years went by, moisture and cold worked their way into the crevice, and, at last, the slab of stone that was my cheek fell away, leaving me lopsided and deformed.

When our eyes met, we instantly saw in each other the loneliness that comes from being truly ugly. We both knew that, in this world, if you are not beautiful, if you are merely simple and plain, people look away. But if you are truly ugly, they look away at first. And then, when they think you do not notice, they turn back and stare.

In the next few years, while the hunchback grew up, he and I spent many hours together, his arms around my shoulders, the warmth of his cheek pressed against the gray stone of mine, as we stared, in lonely silence, out over the streets of the city.

It was then that I came to understand the incredible pain that humans suffer when they are not accepted by their own kind. Even though I am made of stone, it was enough to make me weep.

CHAPTER TWO

❦ The Festival of Fools ❦

ON JANUARY 6, 1482, WHEN QUASIMODO WAS twenty years old, the people of Paris crowned him the King of Fools. This is how it happened:

Here in France, the sixth of January is a double holiday: On this day we celebrate both the holy rite of the Epiphany and the folk holiday known as the Festival of Fools. After Mass, there is a huge bonfire, a maypole, a parade, and then a night of singing, dancing, and drinking, all of which helps the people of Paris forget the chill and gloom of winter.

It was on this festive day that Quasimodo chose to venture into the streets for the first time in his adult life. No one, not even I, saw him step from the safety of the church into the milling crowd that filled the great square of Notre Dame.

At first, Quasimodo passed unnoticed. But then, as he slipped along the walls of the church and stepped out into the open, people shrieked and backed away. Some of the braver ones laughed and tossed insults in his direction.

"He is a demon," shouted a ragged beggar.

"No," said his companion, who had a bandage over one eye, "even I can see that he is an ape dressed in men's clothing."

"You are both fools," said the woman beside them. "That is the hunchback who rings the tower bells. I have seen him on the walls high above. But isn't it strange that he is out among us now?"

"It is not strange at all," a commanding voice said.

The knot of people turned. There, sitting astride his magnificent horse, his armor shining in the winter sunlight, was Phoebus, a handsome young officer in the king's guard.

"This is the Day of Fools," Phoebus said, his fine voice rising above the noise of the crowd, "and perhaps this twisted wreck of man has come to be crowned King of Fools. He is certainly ugly enough!"

The crowd roared with approval. It was their custom each year to choose the ugliest person in Paris to lead the Fools' parade.

Before Quasimodo knew what was happening, a paper crown had been placed on his head and a ragged shawl was tossed over his humped back. He was thrown into an old kitchen chair and hoisted up onto the shoulders of a dozen strong men.

"Friends!" one of the beggars shouted. "Our king has arrived!"

Then the great celebration of Fools began. With the astonished hunchback riding high above the crowd, a noisy, rollicking parade began twisting its way through the streets along the Seine River.

Quasimodo struggled at first, trying to slip away. But even with his great strength, he was not able to twist free from the hands of the rowdy crowd. At last, holding firm to the bouncing chair, I saw him throw back his head and laugh, showing his misshapen teeth.

"He is the finest Fool ever!" someone shouted.

The hunchback did not know that the people were making fun of him. He only knew that, for the first time in his life, he was greeted with smiles and laughter.

At last the cavalcade returned to the square and the kitchen chair was set down before the church like a throne. The street Gypsies came out to perform for the King of Fools and his court of commoners.

Quasimodo howled with delight when he saw the jugglers and the magicians. He also enjoyed the puppeteers and the clowns. He laughed until his good eye was flooded with tears and his belly ached. Acrobats and musicians, fortune-tellers and dog trainers performed for the delighted crowd. And then, with an eerie suddenness, the people in the square fell silent.

Somewhere, there was the jingling of a tambourine. Then, all at once, there she was—a slim maiden dressed in colorful Gypsy clothing, dancing about like a whirlwind.

One of the street merchants had spread an old Persian carpet on the rough cobblestones of the square, and now the Gypsy girl used this as her stage. Her eyes flashed with a dark fire; her delicate limbs moved with an almost supernatural grace, like the branches of a willow tree, waving in the wind. Her jet-black hair rose and fell across her bare shoulders, like waves caressing the shoreline.

Even though she was only fifteen years old, every man in the crowd was instantly captivated by her beauty. Every woman was instantly jealous of her charms. And as for Quasimodo, he had never seen such a lovely creature. His heart went out to her.

But her dancing steps and the enchanting music of her tambourine had attracted the attention of another man, one far different from the commoners.

"You are a witch!" the man shouted. "You do the work of demons. I will not allow you to disgrace this holy place with your vile and shameless dancing!"

Everyone turned and looked. There, on the edge of the crowd, was the red-robed priest, Claude Frollo. He was tall and thin, his bald head rising above the others. His arm was extended, his long, bony finger pointed straight at the girl, who had now stopped dancing and was staring, openmouthed, at her accuser.

"Guards," Frollo shouted, "seize this foul woman!"

But before the king's guards could move, the girl slipped away and vanished into the crowd.

It was then that Frollo's eyes fell on Quasimodo, who sat on his makeshift throne with stooped shoulders and downcast eyes, the ridiculous crown still perched on his head. The priest strode up to the hunchback and snatched away the crown.

A moment before, the poor creature had been King

of Fools. Now he was once again the adopted servant of Frollo, a prisoner of the great church that stood at the head of the square.

Frollo pointed sternly to the entrance of Notre Dame. The King of Fools rose from his chair and, like a dog about to be beaten, made his way through the crowd, toward the doors of our cathedral.

I watched the commoners in the square. For a few moments they looked silently after their king. Then they turned and, shrugging to one another, went on to other entertainments.

The Festival of Fools had only begun.

CHAPTER THREE

❧ Witchcraft and Madness ❧

I HAVE TOLD YOU THAT THE ARCHDEACON, Claude Frollo, was a tormented man. But the incident with the Gypsy girl added one more twist to our story.

The rats have told me that he spent the rest of the festival day in his chambers, behind the thick stone walls of Notre Dame. There he lay on his bed and stared glassy-eyed at the ceiling. They say the room was lit only by the stub of a flickering candle.

I cannot say for certain what was going on in his mind, but I can guess. I think that Frollo, like the other men in the square, had fallen under the spell of the Gypsy girl. And I think his attraction to her frightened him. But his fear and fascination were soon translated into action.

Frollo took to the streets that night, slipping dark-caped and grim-faced through the festive crowd. Quasimodo trailed meekly behind, still aching from the beating the priest had given him that morning.

I suppose Frollo told himself he was on church business. He may have convinced himself that he was only searching for the girl so he could bring her to trial for the crime of witchcraft. But this was not his real motive.

I know now that what he most wanted was to possess this girl, to have her totally within his power, so that he could hold her roughly by her bare shoulders and look her full in the face, meeting her dark and dancing eyes with the smoldering light of his own. This was the only way he could understand the strange power she had over him.

When Frollo was a young man, he turned his back on the troublesome feelings that arose when a woman passed him on the street, brushed against his clothing, or sat too near him in the church pews.

Instead, he gave himself up to the white light of God, purging himself of earthly desires. Through willpower and denial and constant prayer, he had conquered the demons who carried lustful thoughts—or at least he thought he had.

But that day, in the square, when Esmeralda came dancing into his vision, the demons returned. The walls he had built against the world of women came tumbling down. And, no matter how hard he tried, he could not rebuild them. With a combination of dread and desire, the priest left the safety of the church and plunged into the fleshy, noisy crowd.

Frollo found her easily. She was performing for the crowd just a block from the church, in the Square de Grève, which I can see very well from my perch. The square was not normally known for festivity. It was a grisly place where a hangman's scaffold rose rough-hewn and cruel from the cobblestones. Common criminals and raving heretics were painfully executed there, their thrashing legs dancing a few feet above the pavement as their necks were twisted and broken by a rough-spun rope.

The girl had already begun her performance when Frollo and the hunchback slipped into the milling crowd. She was not dancing this time. Instead, she had a goat with her. But this was no ordinary goat: it was a snow-white animal with delicate hooves and curving horns.

"Now, Djali," the girl asked, "what time is it?"

The goat tapped its hoof on the street eight times.

"Djali says it is eight o'clock!" she announced.

The crowd gasped.

"It's a miracle!" a woman cried out. "What else can your goat do, Esmeralda?"

"Esmeralda! So that is her name," Frollo thought.

He said it over to himself, just to get the feel of it between his teeth.

The word burned on his tongue like a droplet of molten lead.

Frollo swallowed hard and watched the girl's slim figure as she gestured to her pet.

"My goat can do arithmetic!" Esmeralda said. "Djali, what is three and three added together?"

Instantly, the goat tapped six times on the pavement.

The crowd laughed in surprise and delight. Small coins showered into the tambourine Esmeralda had laid on the street beside her.

"But my goat is even smarter than this," the girl announced. "It can do imitations as well. It can portray the deacon of Notre Dame. Go ahead, Djali, show us the deacon."

With that, the goat balanced on its hind legs and set its face into such a comical and realistic imitation of Frollo's superior that Frollo himself almost joined the laughter of the crowd.

This was too much. Esmeralda's power over him must have filled him with fear. He wanted to get at her. But he would not do it in the open, as he had that morning. He would wait.

In a half hour, the show was over and people, laughing and shaking their heads in amazement, were moving on to other festivities. Esmeralda stooped and began to pick up the coins that lay scattered around her tambourine.

Frollo turned to Quasimodo, taking him by the arm and drawing him out of the darkness. Because of the bell ringer's deafness, the priest had devised a way of communicating through a simple language of hand signs. Frollo had trained the deformed young man, much as a huntsman would train a hunting dog.

Now Frollo pointed at the bending form of the Gypsy girl and made a sign such as you would give to a retrieving dog. The hunchback obeyed. He lumbered across the emptying square, seized the girl by the waist, and threw her over his shoulder. In the sudden violence of that motion, the tambourine spun from her hands, scattering coins across the pavement. The white goat bleated and bolted into the shadows.

But Esmeralda did not go quietly.

"Murder! Murder!" she cried.

Then I saw a speedy horse rider come galloping from the shadows. Apparently Frollo was not the only one who had been lingering in the shadows. The rider easily overtook the bell ringer. He snatched the startled girl from Quasimodo's back and threw her across his saddle. The hunchback took two wobbling steps, stumbled, and fell in the street. The horseman pulled his steed to a thundering stop. Even in the weak light, I could recognize the handsome features of Captain Phoebus.

Phoebus blew on a shrill whistle. A moment later, Quasimodo was surrounded by a dozen of the king's guard, who quickly bound him in ropes.

One of the soldiers held a lantern, which gave off a yellowish, dappled light. In the lantern's glare, I saw Esmeralda sit up gracefully in the saddle. She placed her hands on Phoebus's square shoulders and stared intently into the captain's eyes, just as Frollo must have wished he could stare into hers. I saw the handsome officer place his gloved hand gently against Esmeralda's cheek. I did not hear what he said to her, but I didn't need to. I could see that her face glowed in the flickering light, and I knew that something had moved in her girlish heart.

It must have chilled Frollo to watch all this from the shadows. But he did not come forward to claim the girl in the name of the church, and he did not come to the aid of his servant. Instead, he simply pulled his cape more tightly around him and vanished down a darkened alley.

Meanwhile, the hunchback bellowed like a wounded ox. A crowd of revelers had gathered to watch the commotion. The deformed man fought hard, kicking and biting and straining against the ropes. But even his great strength was futile against such brutal force.

As the guards hauled Quasimodo away, I heard Phoebus shout after them:

"Easy with him, men. That is not your average ruffian! That man is the King of Fools! How far he has fallen in just a few hours!"

How far, indeed. That night, bruised and bewildered, Quasimodo lay on a sodden clump of straw in the stone-walled prison. For him, it had certainly been a memorable Day of Fools.

CHAPTER FOUR

❧ The Court of Miracles ❧

FOR THE SECOND TIME THAT DAY, ESMERALDA had escaped from the clutches of the priest. The captain gallantly offered to escort her home, but the Gypsy girl only shook her head shyly. She slipped from his saddle and walked away with quick steps. Just before she disappeared around the corner, she turned and caught a glimpse of Phoebus wheeling his horse and trotting away.

In the darkness of the street, she heard the bleating of her goat.

"Come here, Djali!" the girl called.

Her pet came frisking out of the shadows. Esmeralda threw her head back and laughed, cradling the goat in her arms.

"Come on, little one," she crooned, "let's go home."

She and Djali slipped away to a place where no church official could follow. This was a part of the city where not even the king's guards would venture after dark.

I am sad to say that I have never been there. Although I cannot see it from my tower, the rats have brought me the tale.

To find the place Esmeralda called home, you

would have to follow the winding streets that lead from the stinking riverbanks of the Seine, back through the garbage-piled alleys and the crumbling walls of the old city, back to an area so destitute that none but the poorest and most desperate of Paris's citizens would claim it as their own.

It was to this shabby corner of town that Esmeralda and Djali hurried, knowing no one would follow them. Here, even though it was growing late and the night had turned windy and cold, people were still outdoors, making the most of the holiday.

They were clustered around several bonfires that had been built directly on the paving stones, in a great square surrounded by ghostly, dilapidated buildings. The firelight danced across the ruined walls, casting strange shadows on the pockmarked plaster, making the entire square seem like a huge, riotous shadow play.

The rats have told me the air that night was filled with the shrill laughter of women and the bellowing curses of men. The sudden outbursts of quarreling drunkards and the boisterous singing coming from a knot of tone-deaf choirmongers made real conversation impossible. Ragged children ran about the fire as women hoisted scalding pots of mongrel stew from the embers.

Dogs barked and fought with the children over scraps of food that fell under the tables that had been set up for the occasion in the great square. Around each table was a knot of dedicated drinkers, each clasping a mug of peasant beer or a tin cup of rancid wine. The sooty smoke of burning furniture filled the sky. It was a circus of smells, sounds, and rough-shorn sights, sights that would shock the nobility of Paris.

It was this loose nation of beggars, thieves, lunatics, and travelers that made up the tribe to which Esmeralda belonged. Her Gypsy band had happened onto the outskirts of Paris about a year before and had quickly fallen in with these people, who, like themselves, had nothing they could call their own. Esmeralda had left her Gypsy band to stay among the unfortunates, eking out a living by performing on the streets.

Clopin Trouillefou, the King of the Beggars, was standing on a barrel by the fire, raising his arms and shouting for silence.

Esmeralda cradled Djali in her arms and moved closer to the welcoming warmth of the bonfire.

"The Court of Miracles is in session!" the big man boomed.

All heads turned in his direction. The shouts and singing stopped. The gales of laughter quieted. People crowded closer, craning their necks to see.

The king was a rough-faced man with a long beard and a huge knife in his belt. His bald head shone in the firelight.

"Welcome, my ragged subjects!" he shouted. A wild cheer went up from the crowd. Encouraged by their attentiveness, the king became almost eloquent for a moment.

"Welcome to this dirty sanctuary," he said, "where the blind see and the crippled walk! Where those who pretend to be blind beggars can tear the patches from their eyes and limping fakers can cast away their crutches, transforming themselves into unholy citizens of the night!"

The square was suddenly filled with lusty cheers and laughter. Revelers with grimy hands and reddened noses raised their drinks in a drunken toast to the king.

As the girl edged closer to the blaze, the king motioned to her.

"Esmeralda," he said kindly, "bring that goat over here. That is a talented animal; I would hate to see it end up in someone's stewpot!"

The girl smiled and sat down by the king, cradling Djali in her lap.

"Now," the king bellowed, "we will begin our activities by hanging this young fellow."

He gestured to a nervous-looking young man who stood awkwardly by the fire.

"What is my crime?" the man protested.

"You are an honest citizen," the king answered.

"But how can that be a crime?" the man asked, his voice rising in fear.

"You are an honest man who has invaded our part of the city. You are not one of us. So we will treat you just as you treat us when we venture into your territory. We apply the same law to you that you apply to us."

"That would be a great waste," the man replied. "My name is Pierre Gringoire. I am a poet. Perhaps you have heard of me. Perhaps I could compose a poem in your honor—"

"Oh, stop all that," the king shouted. "Let yourself be hung and don't make such a fuss about it!"

A few men were already throwing a rope over the limb of a deadened tree that stood nearby and fastening the noose around the poor man's neck.

"Maybe I could become one of you!" the poet shouted hopefully.

The glowing faces of the crowd erupted in laughter.

"It is not so absurd," the young man said. "After all, I am a poet. I am a poor man, like you. I live very simply. My shoes are as worn as any of yours." He lifted one of his feet to demonstrate.

"You want to join us?" the king asked.

"Yes, of course!"

"Bring on the dummy, then," he shouted.

Someone ran into one of the abandoned houses and came out a moment later with a life-sized cloth dummy to which had been sewn hundreds of tiny, tinkling bells.

"We will hang the dummy from this noose and you must pick his purse"—he held up a small leather bag of coins—"from his belt. If you can do this without ringing a single bell, you may become one of us."

"And if I fail?"

"Then you will take the dummy's place at the end of the rope!"

Pierre watched fearfully as the king tucked the purse into the waistband of the lumpy cloth figure.

"What if the wind blows and rings the bells?" he asked.

"Then we will hang you," came the indifferent answer.

The young man took a step closer to the dummy, which had now begun to sway gently in the breeze.

"Oh, I forgot to tell you," the king said, "you must pick the dummy's purse by standing on one foot atop this rickety stool."

The poet could not believe his ears. "That's ridiculous," he said. "You are not being fair. What if I refuse?"

"Then we will hang you," the king said. "Look, you have taken too much of our time already. Are you going to try the test or not?"

"Of course," the man said weakly.

He stepped onto the stool, raised one foot, and reached carefully into the forest of bells that covered the dummy's waist.

But a wind came up, causing the dummy to sway. Pierre began to sway as well. The crowd watched, open-mouthed, as he fought to stay upright. After hanging for an impossibly long moment on the edge of the stool, he lost his battle with gravity and fell backward. In a last effort to save himself, he grasped the dummy for support. But the cloth figure ripped apart in his hands, and Pierre fell, dragging the dummy down with him. He landed in a noisy heap on the pavement, the sound of hundreds of bells ringing like a death sentence in his ears. The square was filled with laughter.

"Hang the rascal," said the king indifferently, then turned back to his mug of beer. Two men stood the shaking poet on top of a barrel and fastened the rope around his neck.

"I can't believe this is happening," the poor man said to himself.

Suddenly Esmeralda was on her feet.

"Wait," she said. "Sire, aren't you forgetting about the woman's right?"

The king raised his eyebrows. "For this fellow?"

"It is our custom," Esmeralda said.

"What is the woman's right?" the poet asked anxiously.

"It is our custom," the king explained. All at once, he excused himself, sneezed into his drink, then wiped his nose with the back of his hand.

"It is our custom," he continued, "before hanging a man, to first ask if there is any woman here who wants him as a husband. That is the only way you can possibly be saved."

The poet squinted into the firelight, searching wildly through the crowd, hoping to find a friendly face.

But no one came forward.

"Well enough," the king said. "Hang him!"

"Wait!" Esmeralda shouted.

Heads turned in her direction.

"I will take him."

The king frowned.

"Are you sure?" he asked. "He looks very thin and frail, worthless to me."

Esmeralda looked up into the man's frightened eyes.

"I am sure," she said.

"Take him down," the king ordered.

The crowd groaned in disappointment.

"You are a lucky man," the king said to Pierre. "This will be your wedding night! I declare a parade in your honor!"

A great cry went up from the milling masses around the bonfires.

Before either of the newlyweds could move, the rowdy crowd had raised Esmeralda and Pierre onto their shoulders, carried them once around the square, then deposited them on the steps of a ruined building.

Esmeralda took the poet by the hand and pulled him inside, closing the door behind them.

Somewhere in the square, a dog began to howl.

CHAPTER FIVE

❧ A Wedding Night ❧

WHEN I FIRST HEARD THIS STORY, I WAS AS PUZZLED as Pierre must have been. Why would Esmeralda, who was sought after by so many men, willingly marry herself off to such an unlikely specimen as Pierre Gringoire? To find the answer, we must listen to the rat's story:

Inside the crumbling building, down a darkened hallway, Esmeralda had made a home for herself and her goat in a small room. This was where she brought Pierre. The room didn't even have a proper door, just a sheet of ragged canvas tacked along the top of the doorframe. Esmeralda pushed her way inside and held the cloth out of the way, motioning for the poet to join her.

"What can I do to repay you?" Pierre asked when he and Esmeralda were alone.

She said nothing. She struck a spark in the darkness and caught it on a piece of charred cloth. Then she blew it into flame and used it to light the wick of a stubby candle that sat on a nearby table.

The warm light filled the cold room. It was poorly furnished.

In the corner was a roll of cloth that served as

Esmeralda's bed. Pierre could see that the floor was covered with straw.

"Is this where you live?" he asked.

Esmeralda nodded, "Sometimes."

Just then there was a strange clomping sound on the floorboards out in the hallway. A moment later Djali poked its head through the cloth curtain and slipped inside, making itself comfortable on a pile of straw beside Esmeralda.

Pierre started to say something, then waved the thought away. In a night of strange occurrences, this must have seemed like just one more bizarre detail. Instead, he moved ahead to what was on his mind.

"I am glad to be your husband," Pierre said, "and not just because you saved my life. You see, I have seen you dancing in the square. I have even placed coins in your tambourine. But I must warn you, I have no great fortune with which we can begin our lives together."

"I do not need a husband," Esmeralda said simply. "I am only fifteen years old, much too young to marry. And besides, I am already in love with a man, a man I hope will marry me someday."

"May I ask who this lucky man might be?"

Esmeralda's eyes shone brightly.

"Phoebus is his name. He is the captain of the king's guards. He was the one who saved me tonight from that horrible hunchback."

Pierre smiled. "But, Esmeralda, how can you love

him? You know nothing about him: Only that he rides a horse and dashes about and blows his whistle in the dark. What kind of man is this?"

"I know a great deal about him," she said dreamily. "I have often watched him on patrol in the streets. I have seen that he is kind and good and strong. He is the kind of man who would protect a girl such as me. He could protect me in a way that no poet can."

"That is an unkind thing to say," Pierre replied sadly. But then he brightened. "Listen, you have saved my life and I will always be grateful for that. If you will not allow me to be your husband, perhaps we can be friends."

"Perhaps."

"Then tell me, why did you speak up for me?"

Esmeralda stared at the flickering candle.

"Our people can sometimes be cruel," she said. "And there are times when they do not always think about what they do. You must understand, life is hard for us. We have nothing. We cannot own property or be honorably employed. We are insulted and persecuted no matter where we go. Did you see how that horrible priest tried to turn the crowd against me today?"

"But, of course," Pierre said. "You are an enemy of the Church. You are a Gypsy."

"We do not like that name," Esmeralda said bitterly. "It is given to us by people who want to wipe us from the face of the earth."

Pierre nodded. "As a man whose trade is words, I can respect what you are saying. It is important to call something by its proper name. All right then, what do you like to be called?"

Esmeralda pulled her blanket around her shoulders and reached out to scratch Djali between the ears.

"We call ourselves 'the traveling people.'"

"But you are not one of their kind," the poet observed. "You speak French and you have the fair skin of a Parisian."

When he said that, Esmeralda's eyes grew even sadder.

"Yes," she said quietly, "you are right. I am not a true wanderer. I was born to a widowed Frenchwoman who lived on the outskirts of Paris. They say our band was camped in the chalk pits outside the town of Reims when my mother brought me out to see the Gypsies and have my palm read. I was just a small baby then, and they predicted great things for me. My mother became excited. That night, after she took me home, she ran to tell one of her friends.

"It was then that the traveling people took me and hid me away. While Mother was searching for me, the traveling band slipped away in the dark.

"They were kind to me. They raised me to dance and make merry and live by my wits. But I cannot dispute what you say. I was not born a wanderer."

"How do you know all this?" the poet asked.

"The woman in our band who raised me died last year. She had always been healthy, but there was something about this city that did not agree with her. We had just come to Paris after many years of wandering. But there were illnesses here that we did not know. There were fevers that our women could not cure. As she was dying, she gave me this—"

Esmeralda reached down into the neckline of her dress and drew out a green cloth bag that hung by a cord around her neck.

"She said this bag would lead me back to my true mother, if I should choose to search for her."

The poet's eyes grew wide. He had become engrossed in her story.

"Will you show me what is in the bag?" he asked. "Or would this be asking too much?"

"No," Esmeralda said, "I don't know why, but I trust you. I will show you."

Esmeralda fumbled for a moment with the cord, then drew forth a tiny cloth shoe.

"This was mine," she said simply. "The other shoe fell off my foot when the traveling people took me from my mother's house. If she has kept the shoe, as I have, for all these years, perhaps I can find her someday."

"Astonishing," Pierre said. "If there is anything I can do to help you, I promise that I will."

"That is kind."

"Esmeralda—by the way, I have wondered about your name. It sounds Spanish. What does it mean?"

The girl smiled for the first time. "It means emerald."

"Ah," Pierre said, nodding, "a precious stone. You are well named, Esmeralda. I am glad to be your friend."

And with that, he settled down into the straw and drew his coat around him for a blanket. He yawned loudly.

"Forgive me," he said, "I have had a long and very trying day." Then he sighed, closed his eyes, and fell instantly asleep.

Outside the streets had grown quiet. Even on this night of festivities, the city eventually wore itself out and fell into slumber.

Esmeralda slept in her blanket, cradling Djali for warmth.

Pierre Gringoire slept on the thin straw, perhaps dreaming of this strange wedding night.

Quasimodo shuddered as he snored in his dungeon.

But there was one man still awake. Claude Frollo lay in his warm bed in the depths of Notre Dame, tossing and turning. I can only guess what images danced through his mind. For him, sleep did not come for a very long time.

CHAPTER SIX

❧ The Palace of Justice ❧

I AM SADDENED BY THIS STORY, SADDENED AND sometimes amused. It seems to me that most human stories are this way—a mixture of laughter and tears. But what I am about to tell you does not simply make me sad—it fills me with outrage. I suppose I should be used to it by now, but I am still horrified by the depth of cruelty that one human is capable of inflicting upon another.

The rats have told me that Quasimodo was brought to trial in the Palace of Justice the morning after the festival. They say the courtroom was quite crowded, crowded with people who had committed some real or imagined crime during the Day of Fools. It was no coincidence that all of the accused were poor people. Apparently, the wealthy were free to make fools of themselves without fear of penalty.

The courtroom was unheated on that January morning. When the officials spoke, their words hung as clouds of breath, making them feel important and almost immortal. The poor people breathed as well, breathed and coughed, taking in the musty air of the courtroom. As they waited to be tried, they shuffled their feet and blew on their hands to stay warm.

But the judge did not shiver. In fact, he was not even there. He was still home in his warm bed, sleeping soundly under a goose-down quilt. He did not think it was necessary to arise to attend to the wretched prisoners. So the court went on without him.

The cases that morning were tried by the assistant deputy of justice, a small, self-important man who insisted on being called Master Florian. Florian was quite old, dim-witted, and had a poor grasp of the law. Otherwise he was an excellent judge. Oh, I almost forgot to tell you—he had one other difficulty. He was stone-cold deaf.

The absurdity of having a judge who was unable to hear the defendant's pleas was not lost on the common people who crowded the court. But they did not expect the rulings of the Palace of Justice to be just. They knew, deep in the marrow of their shivering bones, that the real purpose of the court was not to learn the truth but to deliver punishment, with a swiftness and severity that would strike fear into the hearts of every citizen.

Florian was not inexperienced. Because the judge was often absent from the court, Master Florian had tried many cases and felt completely secure in his role. He had a system that worked fairly well: He would read over the clerk's report, taking careful note of the defendant's name, age, and occupation.

He would then ask the poor creature these three questions. Nodding sagely, he would write down the answers, copying them from the document he had been given.

Then Florian would read the charges and give the defendant a few moments to respond. After pretending to listen, he would read the poor wretch his sentence and sit gravely as he was whisked away to receive his punishment.

As you may have guessed, no commoner was ever found innocent in Master Florian's court. Florian's method made the beggar king and his Court of Miracles seem almost compassionate.

Quasimodo was still shivering with cold and rubbing the sleep from his eyes when he was brought before Master Florian. Tied in ropes, with a burly guard standing on each side of him, he looked like a bewildered rabbit caught in a trap.

Before Quasimodo was brought in, one of the guards gruffly told him what he must do. The bell ringer could read the guard's lips enough to understand that he was expected to respectfully state his name, age, and occupation.

The assistant judge was seated at a long wooden table, writing in a leather-bound book with a bedraggled quill pen. The clerk of the court, a nervous man with long, thin fingers and chattering teeth, sat nearby with a dripping pen and stack of yellowed papers, ready to record the proceedings of the trial.

"What is your name?" Master Florian asked, without looking up from his papers.

Quasimodo was silent. He was staring down at the floor and was not aware that the judge had spoken to him.

There was a short, uncomfortable silence in the courtroom.

"Quasimodo, eh? A strange name. Am I pronouncing that correctly?" Florian said, copying the bell ringer's name in his book.

Quasimodo was silent.

"I thought so," Master Florian said.

"What is your age?" Florian continued, unaware of his mistake.

Still the hunchback said nothing.

In the silence that followed, one of the guards poked Quasimodo in the side.

When the hunchback cried out in surprise and pain, the judge nodded.

"That is good. Twenty years old," Master Florian said, writing as he spoke.

At this, the commoners began whispering among themselves.

"Silence!" one of the guards barked.

"What is your occupation?" Florian asked.

With an air of confusion, Quasimodo squinted at the magistrate. He had not seen Master Florian's lips move. But he knew from the way the old man's pen was poised above the paper that he was expected to say something.

"My name is Quasimodo," he blurted out.

The commoners erupted in laughter. But Florian did not hear them.

"Very well," the judge said, unaware of the spectacle he was making of himself. Then, to make matters worse, Florian turned to the clerk and asked, "Have you written down everything the defendant has said so far?"

The clerk nodded meekly. By now, the visitors to the court were barely containing their laughter. But Florian never noticed, forging ahead.

"You are accused of three crimes: creating a disturbance, stealing a woman, and resisting arrest. As I am sure you recognize, the third crime is the most severe. What do you have to say in your defense?"

The guard again poked Quasimodo.

"I am twenty years old," the poor man said.

Florian nodded thoughtfully, writing in his book.

By now the courtroom was filled with peals of laughter. The guards shouted for silence. The threat of violence was sufficient to bring the courtroom back to a semblance of order.

Still writing furiously, Florian declared, "This man's testimony is completely unbelievable. In all my years of jurisprudence, I have never heard such an impudent and impertinent display of malfeasance and misconduct. Because of his complete disregard for the sanctity of the law and his total disrespect for the God-given authority of this court, I hereby sentence him to receive twenty lashes on the whipping platform in the Square de Grève. Afterward he is to be turned on the pillory and subjected to public humiliation for a full hour."

The clerk, hoping to inject some appearance of fairness into the process, bent his mouth to the old man's ear and said loudly, "Sir, this man is deaf."

An astonished look swept across Master Florian's face.

"In that case," he intoned, "have him kept on the pillory for an extra hour."

Quasimodo was led away. The absurdity of the trial had escaped him entirely. He knew only that his nose was running, his feet were freezing, and the ropes cut cruelly into his wrists and ankles, making it hard for him to walk. Wild-eyed, he searched the crowd for a familiar face. But he did not see the man he was searching for. He wondered when Claude Frollo would come to save him.

CHAPTER SEVEN

❧ The Whipping ❧

As I have mentioned before, the Square de Grève is within sight of my perch here on the towers of Notre Dame. Many times, I have watched public executions and floggings there, but none as strange as the one I saw that day.

On the morning following the Festival of Fools, the square looked as if the residents of Paris had emptied their trash bins directly onto the streets. The wind kicked about in the square, scattering the discarded papers and cast-off clothing left behind by the revelers. I have often thought there are few things as dismal as the sight of a festival street the morning after the festivities have ended.

But, for the common people, the festivities were not at an end. Quasimodo's punishment would provide an excuse to prolong the carnival for one more day.

Even though Quasimodo's pillorying was not to begin until noon, a large crowd began gathering in the square at about ten o'clock. Word of the ridiculous trial had spread quickly. With that combination of boredom and cruelty that the people of Paris have perfected to a fine art, the commoners had come to see the hunchback writhe under the whip.

The pillory is a cruel instrument of torture. Let me describe it as best I can, because unless you understand the design of this device, you will not fully absorb what happened next.

The pillory is a circular wooden stage, set on top of a cube of masonry, about ten feet above the street. A rude set of wooden stairs leads from the ground to a small platform, which almost touches the edge of the stage.

The unfortunate victim is hauled up these stairs and chained to the stage, kneeling, with his hands tied behind his back. By turning a crank on the underside of the platform, the tormentors cause the small stage to revolve, so that the spectators on all sides may see the prisoner's face and revel in his agony.

This practice is referred to as "turning a criminal." To make the punishment more severe, the magistrate can direct that the prisoner have his ears cut off with a sharp knife or be flogged with a whip.

For Quasimodo, of course, it was to be the whip. And such a whip: attached to the hardwood handle were nine strands of braided leather, tipped with splinters of sharpened steel. The man who was to wield this hideous instrument was no amateur. He was the king's master torturer, Pierrat Torterue.

When the populace was assembled, the king's guards brought Quasimodo out into the square, stripped him to the waist, and tied him to the wheel. The hunchback shivered in the sudden cold. He looked about with his one good eye, squinting in the glare of the bright winter sun. He did not see Claude Frollo in the ocean of dirty and curious faces peering up at him from the cobblestones.

People craned their necks to see the half-naked body of the deformed man. Even though it was a common belief that looking upon a deformed person could bring bad luck, the revelers temporarily suspended this rule and stood gaping, taking in the full horror of his ugliness. Their eyes wandered mercilessly over his arching hump, his protruding chest, and his stooped, hairy shoulders.

It was a strange bit of irony that, just the day before, these same people had crowned the bell ringer their king, and now, because of a cruel twist of fate, they were witnessing his punishment as a common criminal.

Master Torterue climbed the wooden stairs that led to the platform. In his right fist, he held the terrible whip. With his left hand, he slowly rolled up his right sleeve. The torturer stamped his foot.

Working the crank, Torterue's assistants caused the circle to turn. Quasimodo looked about him like a bewildered calf being led to slaughter. As his bowed and naked back was presented to Master Pierrat, the torturer raised his right arm and brought the whip down sharply across the poor man's back.

Quasimodo arched and threw back his head, his mouth opening in pain and surprise. But no sound came out.

The crowd roared, urging the whip man on. The sharp-edged blows rained down on Quasimodo's back. Soon his whitened skin seemed like a huge map, where rivers ran red with blood and mountain ranges rose, jagged and scarred, from the slope of his great shoulders to the base of his twisted spine.

After the twentieth stroke, Master Pierrat stopped to catch his breath, shaking the blood from his whip. The torturer had worked himself into a perfect fury, turning the helpless figure before him into a mass of reddened meat, but still the prisoner had not cried out.

In the sudden quiet that accompanied the creaking of the wheel and the hard breathing of the torturer, a beggar shouted, "You are wasting your time, Master Pierrat! He is a beast who can feel no pain!"

The whipmaster turned and faced the crowd. His face and chest were speckled with blood. "He is not a beast," Pierrat shouted; "he is a demon. I know he cannot be saved. But, by God, he will cry out!"

With a fury that astonished everyone, he doubled the penalty by laying another twenty lashes across Quasimodo's back. But the bell ringer did not cry out. Instead, his head fell forward and he slumped down on the platform like a pile of misshapen clay. It was only the chains and the binding ropes that held him upright.

At last, an officer from the guard nodded to Master Pierrat. Reluctantly, the torturer coiled his whip and, walking unsteadily, descended the stairs. The two young men who were the torturer's apprentices brought a bucket of water and washed the hunchback's wounds, smearing an ointment of blackened pine pitch into the ragged cuts. Then they threw a yellowed cloth over his massive back and left him to kneel, dazed and dumb, on the horrible wheel.

The crowd buzzed with astonishment. They had never seen any creature, man or beast, take such brutal punishment with so little display of pain.

The officer mounted the platform and raised his hand for silence.

Suddenly the great square was still. The only sound was the wind, casting dried pieces of paper against the walls of the buildings.

The soldier produced an hourglass from his coat and placed it on the edge of the platform. "In order that justice should be fully satisfied," he announced, "the prisoner will remain on the pillory for two full hours of public humiliation. God rest the king!"

I thought then that the crowd might have seen enough pain and hardship for one day. But I was wrong. If anything, the whipping had only inflamed the hatred the street people felt toward Quasimodo.

"He is on the pillory now," a dirty-faced girl shrieked. "Perhaps next week we shall see him on the gallows!"

The crowd roared its approval.

A hailstorm of insults was cast on Quasimodo then. But words were not the only things thrown in his direction. People bent and plucked stones or soggy clods of mud from the street and hurled them at him.

Of course, the insults were wasted on the hunchback. He could not hear them. Even the sharp whack of the paving stones against his body was only a minor irritation. I could see then that he was long past the threshold of physical pain. It was difficult to watch this savage display of cruelty. But, you must understand, as a gargoyle, I had no choice. Because a gargoyle cannot close his eyes.

Just when it seemed that I could stand it no longer, I saw someone climbing the stairs to the pillory. It was not the whipmaster or the officer. It was Esmeralda.

The crowd was astonished. They dropped their taunts and their cobblestones. Everyone wanted to see what would happen next. Everyone knew it was the demon's crime against this girl that had brought him to the pillory. Now, perhaps, she would take her revenge by pounding him with her fists as he knelt, helpless and bound. But Esmeralda did not strike the hunchback. Instead she took a gourd canteen from the belt at her waist, poured a little water into her cupped palm, and held it to Quasimodo's trembling lips.

The hunchback stared at her through a single, bloodshot eye. Then he understood. In the midst of such savagery, he glimpsed a ray of simple kindness.

Moving his lips, which were reddened with blood, he drank gratefully, for his thirst was powerful.

While he drank, he wept. Tears streamed from his

good and bad eyes, and his body shook with sobs. He cried out loudly in gratitude, in a voice that seemed to shake the building stones. Esmeralda had accomplished what Master Torterue could not. She had given the poor man a reason to cry out.

The crowd fell still in amazement, with the exception of one old woman, whose voice rose above the stone silence of the street.

"Curse you, daughter of Egypt! Curse you!"

CHAPTER EIGHT

❧ A Lost Child ❧

THE OLD WOMAN'S VOICE HAD COME THROUGH the bars of a window in Roland Tower, on the edge of the square.

"Hang her," the old hag wailed; "hang her and the devilish one together."

But before the crowd could pick up the chant, the officer of the guard stepped forward and ordered his men to unchain the hunchback and lift him down the stairs. They led him back to the doorway of our church, untied him, and left him slumped against the threshold of the great doors of Notre Dame. I watched the bell ringer crawl inside the sanctuary of our church, free from the shouts and insults of the street.

Meanwhile, the Gypsy girl had vanished.

With nothing else to amuse them, the crowd began to melt from the great square, turning back to their lives. It was a cold January afternoon, the sky was clouding, and spring was still several months away.

I watched the narrow window of Roland Tower and saw a withered pair of hands grip the iron bars. A moment later, the thin, wrinkled face of Sister Gudule appeared in the opening.

Sister Gudule was a familiar figure in the Square

de Grève. She was a beggar woman who lived in an unheated chamber at the base of the stone tower. Through a series of misfortunes, she had ended up old and penniless on the streets of Paris.

For the last fifteen years, she had claimed this crumbling chamber as her home and had shut herself inside, looking out at the world through a grate of iron bars that covered the window. How she stayed alive in the terrible cold, I will never know.

The locals took her to be something of a saint because she spent all of her waking hours on her bony knees in the chamber, praying with an intensity that was almost supernatural. She lived by the charity of others. Because she was so destitute and because people were a little afraid of her, they kept her alive with small gifts of food and drink, a crust of black bread, or a pitcher of sour wine.

"Gypsy girl must die!" she shrieked through the bars.

But people scarcely noticed her, as they passed out of the square.

I cannot tell you very much about Sister Gudule. But I can tell you this: she hated Gypsies.

From the little that I could learn, her baby girl had been stolen fifteen years before. She had no husband and, as far as I knew, no children, except for the one who was stolen. The pigeons who roost by her window tell me that she had the child very late in life and lavished the newborn with love and affection. As we say in Paris, "An old maid makes a young mother."

From what the birds tell me, the child became the center of her life. Then one evening, she heard that a band of Gypsies was camped out by the chalk pits on the edge of town. Full of foolish superstition, she took her baby out to the camp to have the infant's palm read.

The old Gypsy woman who glanced into the baby's tender hand predicted great things for the girl, saying she would eat at the tables of kings, and so forth. The woman became so excited that when she returned to her apartment that evening she left the baby for a moment to run down the hall and tell her neighbor the happy news.

But when she returned, her precious baby girl was gone. Although she searched wildly up and down the streets and alleys, she couldn't find any sign of the girl. That night, the caravan left town.

When the distraught woman returned to her apartment toward morning, she saw a kicking bundle on her doorstep. Flooded with joy and relief, she dashed over to the child and threw back the blanket. But this was not her daughter—this was a boy, horribly deformed, with twisted legs and a curved spine. The Gypsies had left a monster in exchange for her sweet, tender girl.

In the last hour before dawn, she bundled the boy up and carried him to the steps of Notre Dame. The rest you know.

For fifteen years, Sister Gudule grieved for the

missing child. Holed up in the chamber of Roland Tower, she squatted on the stones, cursing the dark-skinned Gypsies and praying endlessly for the return of her daughter.

The sight of the Gypsy girl that afternoon had inflamed her to the boiling point. She paced her cell, muttering to herself and stroking the whitened hairs that sprouted on her withered chin.

If she could have called thunderbolts down from the sky, she vowed, she would have done it. She would have incinerated the Gypsy girl on the spot.

But no thunderbolts had come. In spring, thunderstorms come to Paris. But spring was still weeks away, and the winter wind smelled like snow.

CHAPTER NINE

❧ A Secret Meeting ❧

THE TIME OF THUNDERSTORMS CAME AT LAST. In March, during the great storms, the roof of Notre Dame leaks. The workmen do their best to seal the cracks in the roof by filling them with molten lead, but it is a losing battle. Our church was built two hundred years before the events of this story. I was made shortly after. The seasons have not been kind to either of us.

After his adventures at the Festival of Fools, Quasimodo did not venture again from the safety of our church. Instead, he stayed with me, here in the bell tower. He rang his bells, but not as sweetly as before.

I suppose that Quasimodo always hoped his fellow church dwellers would welcome him as a brother and a friend. But now, when the one man he trusted had treated him so cruelly, he abandoned this hope and became solitary and reclusive.

The wounds on his back healed during the quiet winter months.

But I could see that his inner wounds still festered. In the slow, still chambers of his mind, I think he understood that Frollo had betrayed him. He did not know why. But there were many things the deaf man did not understand, and this was only one more mystery.

Now and then, we would spot Esmeralda and her goat performing in the street far below. Whenever this happened, Quasimodo would stop what he was doing and sit beside me on the edge of the roof, staring down at the girl for as long as she remained in sight.

From that height, she was just a wash of color and a flash of silver as she danced. But, if we were very quiet, we would hear the music of her tambourine drifting up from the square. It was a fine sight to see her dancing so gaily on the cobblestones.

Quasimodo never spoke during these times. But he sighed now and then. I can only guess what he was thinking.

My friend was not the only one who watched Esmeralda. There were three others who took a special interest in her.

Pierre Gringoire, as a poet and a sincere lover of beauty, had remained Esmeralda's husband. The truth was, they were not husband and wife at all. Esmeralda was right; she was too young to marry, so they lived together as brother and sister. Finding acrobatics more profitable than poetry, Pierre joined the Court of Miracles and made a passable living by performing on the street, balancing chairs on his chin and eating strips of wood tipped with fire.

Captain Phoebus had not forgotten Esmeralda either. Since the night when she had perched on his saddle and placed her hands on his shoulders, he had been captivated by the memory of their brief meeting. But their paths had crossed very rarely. Besides, with so many women begging for the handsome captain's attentions, he was easily distracted.

Meanwhile, Claude Frollo had fallen further into the depths of madness. In the dark days of winter, he spent many an hour with charms and spells, trying to rid himself of his unexplainable attraction to the Gypsy girl.

At last, when all his magic had failed, he decided to have the girl executed, putting an end to his torment. A hanging would be easy to arrange, he reasoned. The Church had the power to seize and destroy anyone who dabbled in the black arts.

Frollo had often seen Esmeralda and her goat performing in the square. That was surely witchcraft; no one would deny it. But he did not want to bungle things as he had on the Day of Fools. Instead, he waited.

His chance came quite unexpectedly, on a warm evening in March, when he was standing in the doorway of Notre Dame, brooding over his misery and watching the first stars come out.

I saw Captain Phoebus appear in the square, riding on his evening patrol. Not far away, I saw the Gypsy girl and her goat, returning from a day of performing. I could see that their paths would cross.

"Esmeralda," the captain called out.

The girl smiled.

"You remember my name," she said brightly, taking a few steps toward him.

"Yes, of course. And do you remember mine?"

The girl blushed. "Yes. Even Djali remembers your name. Watch this—"

Phoebus swung down from his horse and let the reins dangle from his gloved hand. He watched as the lovely girl pulled a handful of wooden blocks from her traveling bag and tossed them on the ground in front of the goat.

"Go ahead, Djali," she said, "show the captain what you can do."

Without hesitation, the goat used its front hooves to move the blocks around, arranging them in a neat row.

When the captain bent for a closer look, he saw that each block had a letter carved into it. When he looked even closer, he saw that the letters spelled "Phoebus."

"Esmeralda," he said, "this is astonishing."

"Yes," the girl laughed, "isn't it wonderful?"

Then she added shyly, "It took me weeks to teach it to do that."

"To spell my name?"

"Yes."

"But why?"

"Because, sir—" Then she hesitated, shaking her head as if she had lost her nerve.

The handsome captain stroked his mustache.

"You don't have to be afraid, you can tell me," he said.

"Because," Esmeralda blurted out, "because, sir, I love you."

The captain laughed. It was a jaunty, gracious laugh, designed to put the girl at ease.

"Listen," I heard the captain say, as if he was thinking of it for the first time, "I know a lovely place down by the river, just a few blocks away. Bring your goat, and we'll sit and watch the stars."

"Do you think it would be all right?" Esmeralda asked. "I mean, aren't you supposed to be patrolling the streets, making sure that people are safe?"

The captain smiled. "That is precisely what I am doing, my dear. Now come, and bring that clever animal with you. I must confess, I have always loved goats."

Esmeralda stooped and picked up the wooden blocks, slipping them into her bag. Phoebus led his horse with his left hand and offered the girl his right arm. A moment later, they were walking toward the river. I saw Frollo slip quietly from the doorway of the church and follow them down the street.

The pigeons tell me that they found a secluded place by the river. Phoebus tied his horse to a wooden post. Djali nibbled on some rushes that grew by the river. The soldier drew Esmeralda to a sheltered place in a grove of willow trees. They sat on a wooden bench with a view of the river.

Frollo stood back in the shadows.

"I hope you won't despise me for coming here with you," Esmeralda said.

"Why should I despise you, my dear?"

"Because I am not a fine and honorable woman, like most of the women you know. Because I am just a poor girl with no mother and father, who must look out for herself and live by her wits."

Phoebus smiled. He said nothing.

"I must confess," Esmeralda said, "that I love you very much. I have loved you since the first moment I saw you, riding tall and proud, above the crowd in the square. I know this is foolish of me. I know there are many women who vie for your affections. I know there is very little chance that you would become my champion. But my heart does not understand these practical matters. When I tell my heart this, it only laughs at me. My heart knows only that I want to be yours."

This sudden outpouring of affection caught the captain a little off guard, but he quickly regained his balance.

"Tell me this," he said, twirling his mustache, "what is it about me that you find so attractive?"

Esmeralda laughed. Her eyes sparkled like emeralds.

"You are strong and good and try to help people whenever you can," she said. "You are so different from the common people, who often think only of themselves. Captain," she said, "will you do me a favor?"

"Of course, Esmeralda."

"Would you show me your sword?"

The captain laughed. "You are such a child. Why would you want to see my sword?"

"Because it is yours."

The captain laughed.

"That is reason enough," he said gallantly, drawing his blade from the scabbard. He laid it across her outstretched palms. She marveled at how it glistened in the starlight.

"Be careful," he said, "it is very sharp."

Esmeralda sat, her back straight, the river breezes lifting her hair, the close smell of her rising into Phoebus's nostrils. She smelled of spices and wood fires and fresh bread. Across the water, the lights of Paris glimmered on the rippled surface of the Seine. In the branches of the willow trees, a pigeon cooed, low and mournfully.

At last, Esmeralda handed the blade back to its owner.

"I have a sword as well," she confessed.

"A sword?"

"Well, a dagger, really. Would you like to see it?"

The captain nodded.

Esmeralda pulled up her skirt and drew a knife from a leather sheath attached to her thigh. She placed the blade into Phoebus's outstretched hands.

Now it was the captain's turn to marvel. It was a finely made dagger, with a six-inch blade; a sharp, deadly point; and a small, green emerald set into the handle.

57

"You know it is against the law to carry a concealed weapon in Paris," he said.

"I know that," Esmeralda confessed. "But a woman who travels alone in this city needs protection. If you would be my champion, I would not need a dagger, I would not need to look back over my shoulder as I walk the dark streets."

Phoebus lowered the dagger and laid it on the edge of the bench.

"Let us set aside our swords now, Esmeralda," he said.

"But why?"

"So I can teach you the language of love," he said.

The captain pulled her close, taking her into his arms and searching for her lips in the darkness.

As if guided by some mysterious force, Frollo found himself parting the willow branches and stepping forward. Three quiet steps and he was standing beside the bench. His hand reached out and closed around Esmeralda's dagger.

In a single, smooth motion Frollo raised his arm and brought the dagger down swiftly, sinking it deep into the captain's back, just above the right shoulder blade.

Phoebus cursed and fell forward onto his face, upsetting the bench. Esmeralda scrambled to her feet. In the dim light, she saw the handle of her knife protruding from the fabric of the captain's coat. A wine-dark stain was spreading across Phoebus's back.

The soldier rolled onto his side, groping among his coat buttons. His trembling hand found what it was searching for. He fitted his silver whistle to his lips and blew a shrill blast. Still tethered to the post, the horse snorted and pulled at its reins.

It was only then that Esmeralda noticed the priest, standing still as a statue, among the willows.

A moment later, Esmeralda heard the shouts of two men. The king's guards were on the riverbank.

The soldiers pushed their way through the brush and burst into the clearing. They were breathing hard and had drawn their swords.

"What happened here?" one of the sergeants demanded.

Frollo pointed to the Gypsy girl.

"That witch just stabbed your captain!"

CHAPTER TEN

❧ A Confession ❧

IN THE WEEKS THAT FOLLOWED, THE RATS MADE many visits to the dungeon that lies beneath the Palace of Justice. They say that the Gypsy girl was locked away there, in a cold and dripping cell, far from the light and warmth of the wintry sun.

For Esmeralda, who was accustomed to a healthy regimen of sunlight and music and laughter, the weeks passed slowly in the quiet drabness of her cell. At last, the court agreed to hear her case.

Once the deliberations began, Esmeralda's trial went swiftly.

The evidence against her was overpowering.

Frollo was eloquent in describing the circumstances of the murder.

"When I saw the Gypsy girl casting her spell on the good captain," he told the court, "I followed them. If I could have, I would have warned him. But I could not come to his aid quickly enough. By the time I arrived, she had already stabbed him and was standing over the fallen man, muttering magical incantations."

The charge of witchcraft was just as easy to prove. There were many witnesses who had seen the tricks the girl and her magical goat could perform. And, besides, everyone reasoned, she was a Gypsy.

After Frollo had presented his case, the head judge, the honorable Jacques Charmolue, called for the defendant to be brought up from her cell.

In a few moments, Esmeralda appeared in the doorway of the court, flanked by two rough-handed guards. This was not the gay girl who had brightened the streets of Paris with her dancing and music. This was a weeping, shivering wretch, with blue lips and dirty hair, wearing a stained dress, torn at the shoulder. Her feet were bare and black with dirt.

"Please," Esmeralda said through cold-cracked lips, "please, before you kill me, tell me—is Phoebus still alive?"

"That is of no concern to you," the judge said coldly.

"Have pity on me," she begged. "Tell me if he is still living."

"Very well, then," the judge said dryly, "he is on the point of death, if you must know."

Esmeralda covered her dirty face with her hands and began to sob. It was impossible to tell if she was crying for joy or sorrow.

"Gypsy girl," the judge said solemnly, "you will stand before the court."

Esmeralda straightened herself and wiped the tears from her face.

The judge turned to the bailiff.

"Bring in the other prisoner," he said.

A moment later, a soldier appeared in the door, leading a white goat by a rope.

"Djali!" the girl cried out.

"Take note," the judge said, "the Gypsy has recognized her accomplice."

Esmeralda reached for her pet, but the guards held her firmly. The goat was tied to a bannister near the judge's desk.

It was common in those days for animals to be tried for witchcraft. Church officials were never shy about pointing out the fact that demons and witches could appear in many forms. If the animal had a cloven hoof, so much the better.

"If the court pleases, I will make a short demonstration," Frollo said. He motioned to one of the bailiffs, who brought Esmeralda's traveling bag. Frollo rolled the wooden blocks out onto the floor.

"No, Djali!" Esmeralda shouted.

But she was too late.

Quickly the clever goat shoved the blocks around on the wooden floor of the Palace of Justice, spelling out the name "Phoebus."

The judge arched his eyebrows.

"Very interesting," he said.

Esmeralda hung her head.

"Prisoner," Charmolue said gravely, "you are of the Gypsy race, which is given to evil ways. On the night of March 29, aided by the powers of darkness and the bewitched goat that is now on trial with you, you stabbed Captain Phoebus de Châteaupers. Do you persist in denying it?"

"Yes!" she cried out through her tears, "I deny it."

"Then how do you explain the evidence against you?"

"I can't explain it. I don't understand what you are talking about."

The judge frowned.

"In view of the prisoner's resistance," he said, "I recommend the application of torture to extract a suitable confession. Take her to Master Torterue."

Before Esmeralda could say anything, she was swept off her feet and dragged from the room.

The goat bleated plaintively.

ESMERALDA WAS TAKEN DOWN A WINDING STONE staircase and into a round room filled with frightful-looking instruments. There were chains set into the wall and leather straps that hung from the ceiling. A small fire flickered in an oven. Several metal pokers lay nearby, blackened with fire.

The court clerk set up his papers and inkwell on a small table near the flickering glow of the oven.

Master Torterue, a cruel smile playing at his lips, entered the room. He was wearing a leather apron stained with blood. He motioned to a chair that sat by the fire.

The guards placed Esmeralda in the chair and tied her wrists to its arms.

Just then, Justice Charmolue appeared in the doorway.

Master Torterue smiled thinly.

"Justice, you honor us with your presence," he said quietly.

"I want to assure myself that everything is done properly," the judge said.

Torterue cast his eyes on the trembling form of the girl.

"Everything shall be done properly," he said coldly.

"Prisoner," the judge said, "do you still persist in your denial?"

Esmeralda nodded weakly.

"In that case, we shall have to proceed with our questioning."

"How shall we begin?" the specialist asked.

"We'll begin with the boot," the judge said.

Esmeralda's eyes widened with terror as she felt her foot being placed into a heavy iron vise.

"What a pity," the judge mused, "you will never dance with that foot again."

The torturer had barely begun to tighten the iron jaws of the device when Esmeralda cried out.

"Take it off!" she said.

"Do you confess?" the judge said urgently.

"How can I confess?" Esmeralda asked. "I am innocent."

"Do you deny your crimes?"

"Of course!"

Charmolue nodded to Torterue.

The cruel man tightened the vise. The iron jaws dug into the girl's flesh, pressing mercilessly against the delicate bones of her foot.

Esmeralda threw back her head and screamed.

"Oh, close the door," the judge said irritably. "I don't want the good men of the court to be troubled by this witch's screams."

"I confess!" Esmeralda gasped, "I confess to everything!"

"It is my duty to tell you that you can expect death as a result of your confession."

"I hope so," the girl said, her teeth clenched in pain.

The judge motioned to the clerk. "Come now, write this down," he ordered.

"Gypsy girl," the judge said, "do you confess to the murder of Captain Phoebus?"

"Yes," she said, her voice trembling in agony.

"And do you confess to the practice of witchcraft?"

Esmeralda, her eyes tightly closed, nodded.

"You must speak the word," the judge prompted.

"Yes," she said.

"And do you confess to having the devil's aid in the form of the white goat that is on trial with you?"

Esmeralda said nothing.

"Answer!" the judge thundered.

"Yes," Esmeralda said, choking on her own tears.

"Finish writing all that down, clerk. Master

Torterue, you may remove the boot. Guards, help this young murderer back up to the courtroom. The court will be gratified to know that we acted with all possible gentleness. As far as I can see, no bones were broken."

Esmeralda felt her body being lifted from the chair. Her foot throbbed with a dull ache.

Once they were settled back in the courtroom, the judge frowned at Esmeralda across his long table.

"Gypsy girl," he said, "have you admitted to all the charges of witchcraft and murder?"

"But I thought you said Phoebus was not yet dead," the girl interjected.

"Silence! Answer the question."

"I confess. I'll say anything you like. Just kill me quickly!"

The judge nodded.

"Very well. At noon tomorrow, you shall be taken to the central doorway of Notre Dame, where you shall do public penance with a wax candle weighing two pounds in your hand. From there you shall be taken to the Square de Grève, where you will be hanged on the gallows of the city, along with your wicked goat. May God have mercy on your wretched soul."

Esmeralda closed her eyes. She felt rough hands dragging her away.

CHAPTER ELEVEN

❧ Face to Face ❧

THAT NIGHT FROLLO VISITED ESMERALDA IN HER miserable cell.

He opened the rusty iron door and, carrying a candle lantern, walked into the low room.

Esmeralda squinted painfully in the harsh light.

"Who are you?" she asked.

The priest set the lantern on the floor between them and straightened.

"My name is Dom Claude Frollo," he said.

Suddenly the girl recognized her accuser.

"You are that horrible priest!" she cried. "Go away!"

"You are in no position to order me about," Frollo reminded her. "You are condemned to death."

"Then let me die soon," she said bitterly.

"Do you know why you are here?" he asked.

Esmeralda tried to be brave. But her voice began to break as tears welled up in her eyes. "I used to know," she said miserably, "but now I can't remember."

"You are here because of me," Frollo said. "I brought you here and I can take you out."

Suddenly Esmeralda's eyes grew wide.

"Now I remember! You are the one who stabbed Phoebus!" she said.

Instinctively her hand reached for the dagger at her thigh, but she found the sheath empty. Then the horrible events of the night by the river came tumbling back into memory.

Tears of rage filled her eyes. Esmeralda flung herself at the priest with a suddenness that caught him off guard. She pushed him backward. His boots slipped on the wet floor, and he fell roughly against the crude stone wall. As he fell, his foot caught the lantern, which fell on its side and went out. They were now plunged into perfect darkness.

Like a wildcat, Esmeralda fell on the priest. She bit and kicked him. She pummeled him with her fists. He cursed and cried out in pain, but still she beat him. At last, the priest grabbed her thin shoulders and shook her with such violence that she almost passed out.

In the secret darkness, Frollo began covering her neck with passionate kisses.

"I love you," he moaned.

The Gypsy girl fought him off and scrambled away, flattening herself against the wall of the cell. For a moment, the only sound was the rough and rasping breathing of the two combatants, gathering strength for the next battle.

"Why do you say you love me? Why do you taunt me this way? What do you want from me?" Esmeralda asked. Her voice was hoarse and desperate.

"I am bewitched by you," Frollo said. "Before I saw your dancing form, I was happy—or at least I thought

I was. And then, once I saw you, I knew I wanted to possess you. That feeling is not permitted among priests. So I did my best to purge myself of this desire. But it did not pass. Your dancing whirled in my brain. I felt your spell at work in me. I had to admit that I was powerless before you.

"That is why I tried to have you kidnapped. That is why I followed you and Phoebus to the riverbank. That is why I have condemned you to death—in hopes that this will free me."

"You are the icy hand of death," Esmeralda said coldly.

"Is this some type of spell you are casting on me?" Frollo asked, his voice rising in fear.

"I do not know any spells," Esmeralda shot back.

"Then you are not a student of the black arts?"

"Of course not."

"But you are a Gypsy and everyone knows—"

"That we are masters of witchcraft? It is a lie! Ask yourself: If we really did have the power to command the spirits, would we choose to live in poverty and shame? Would we wander from place to place with no home and no rights? Would we be forced to make our living by dancing in the dirt of the streets?"

"If you are not an enchantress, how do you explain this nameless passion that has come over me?" he asked.

"I cannot explain it," Esmeralda said. "To find the answer, you must look into the darkness of your own heart. I am sure you will find the answer there."

Frollo was silent for a moment.

"I will save you if you will save me," he declared.

"What are you talking about?"

"If you will come away with me and become my lover, then I will see that the death sentence is lifted."

"Never!" Esmeralda spat out. "You killed my Phoebus! You are just an ugly, disgusting man, withered and bald. It is a good thing you are a priest. No woman would have you!"

Frollo rose and felt his way along the wall until he came to the iron door.

"Then die!" he said fiercely. He pushed his shoulder against the door and felt it give way. He slammed it hard against its hinges and slipped the sturdy bolt into place, sealing her into the musty room. A moment later, he was scrambling on hands and knees up the stone stairs, toward the unchained world, far overhead.

Esmeralda slumped against the wall in her cell. This was how she spent her final night in prison.

"I am ready to die," she said in the darkness. No one heard her but the rats, which scurried across the floor, gnawing on the candle Frollo had dropped.

CAPTAIN PHOEBUS WAS NOT DEAD. MEN LIKE HIM are hard to kill. The pigeons tell me he was taken to a hospital outside Paris, where he recovered from his wound rather quickly. In the time he was away, he had completely forgotten about Esmeralda. On the morning of Esmeralda's execution, Phoebus happened to be visiting a beautiful young woman who had a balconied apartment overlooking the Square de Grève.

The birds say he and his new love were drinking wine from crystal glasses when the woman spoke.

"We will be married in three months, Phoebus. Swear to me that you have never loved another woman."

"I swear it," he said, twirling his mustache.

Just then, a great shout went up from the square.

Phoebus frowned at the interruption. "What is all that noise?" he asked.

"They are hanging a witch today," the woman said brightly.

"What is her name?"

"I don't know. There are so many witches nowadays," she said, "they hang them without even knowing their names. You might as well try to know the name of every cloud."

She rose and walked to the balcony.

"Good heavens, Phoebus. Come look at this mob; they are even standing on the rooftops! Look, they are bringing the witch out now. Oh, Phoebus, it's that Gypsy girl—the one who used to perform in the square with that filthy goat!"

Phoebus pushed past her and gripped the balcony railing, staring down into the milling crowd. At last, his eyes fell on the frail form of Esmeralda, being led to the gallows. They were four stories above the street, close enough for the captain to make out the the girl's sorrowful features. The pigeons fluttered about the balcony. They say Pheobus grew red in the face.

"What is it, my dear?" the woman asked.

Phoebus stared, saying nothing.

"Is there something about the execution of this girl that troubles you? Perhaps you have some warm feelings for her," the woman joked, never guessing how close she came to the truth.

"No," Phoebus made himself say, "she is nothing to me."

"Are you quite sure?"

"Yes, of course."

"In that case, stay here," she said haughtily, "and we'll watch till the end."

The captain had no choice.

"As you wish," he said.

The woman laughed brightly.

"I have always loved this apartment," she said; "we have such a grand view of things from here."

Meanwhile the crowd had grown ugly in the street below. When word spread that Esmeralda was to be hanged, the King of the Beggars had taken it as a great insult. He had roused the Court of Miracles and they had crowded into the square, full of ill will toward the judges and priests who hung the members of their tribe so carelessly.

The beggars, cutthroats, and thieves, the acrobats and magicians, even cowardly dreamers like Pierre Gringoire were there, determined to do what they could to prevent this terrible miscarriage of justice.

• • •

I HAD A GRAND VIEW OF THE EXECUTION AS WELL. Having witnessed so many sorrowful deaths in the Square de Grève, I prepared myself to see two more.

Esmeralda and her goat were brought to the gallows in a wooden-wheeled cart drawn by a short-legged Spanish mule. They were lifted up the stairs and placed on the gallows platform, where the executioner was arranging his ropes. I could hear the crowd, roaring like the sound of ocean waves thundering to the shore. A heavily armed contingent of the king's guard ringed the gallows platform.

There were many officials on hand, representatives of both the state and the church. I could see Frollo there in his dark robe, clutching his black book and pacing on the street below the gallows. His eyes seemed to burn with a reddish fire.

Esmeralda glanced wildly about, hoping she could see a way out of this death trap. Then her eyes chanced to wander upward and fastened on the two lovers on the balcony far above.

Suddenly Esmeralda's eyes widened.

"Phoebus," she called out. "My Phoebus, you are alive!"

She turned to the hangman.

"Gentlemen," she said breathlessly, "you can't hang me for murder. Look there, on the balcony, it is Captain Phoebus! He is not dead after all."

But no one took the time to look. No one heard her words or listened to her frantic claims. They had come to see a woman hanged, and by the authority of the king, they were determined to see her hang.

My thoughts suddenly flew to Quasimodo. I wondered how he would react to the horror of this gruesome spectacle. But he didn't appear beside me. In fact, I hadn't seen him since early morning. The thought occurred to me that he might not even know about the trial and might be sleeping in his chamber, unaware of Esmeralda's fate.

Then I spotted him. There was no mistaking the awkward bulk of his twisted form. He was edging his way along a rooftop far above the Square de Grève. I knew it was him. But I couldn't imagine what he was doing in such a dangerous spot. If he fell, I realized, he would land right on top of the city gallows.

Then I noticed that he was tying a length of rope to one of the huge stone columns, a rope such as the workmen use when they want to hang over the side of our church to fix the roof. It wasn't until he gripped the rope and swung over the edge that I realized what he was doing.

A great shout went up from the crowd as Quasimodo slid down the rope like a raindrop down a windowpane. He swung through the officials crowding the dock, knocking the executioner off the platform and down into the crowd. He sprang in among the soldiers and the politicians, felling them with his great fists, toppling them off the edge of the platform. He raged like a mad bull.

The goat bleated and scampered away. Esmeralda turned and took two steps toward the stairway before she was caught around the waist by Quasimodo. Gripping the long rope, the hunchback swung down off the gallows, over the heads of the crowd, and landed on the fabric roof of an awning. There he dropped from the rope and slid down to the street.

Clutching the girl like a rag doll, he pounded across the pavement, knocking over everyone in his path. I saw that he was headed for the main door of the church. A squad of sword-wielding guards and a ragged knot of beggars set out after him. But he was far ahead. He beat them to the doorway and swung the great doors shut behind him, bolting them firmly.

The crowd roared and surged in confusion. They rushed to the square of Notre Dame and stood with their hands shielding their eyes, looking up at the bell tower. A few moments later, I heard Quasimodo's heavy footsteps on the stone stairway. He rushed to the edge of the roof and stood beside me, in full view of the crowd below.

In his arms was the limp body of the Gypsy girl. Quasimodo held her high above his head, so the whole city could see. In a great voice, a voice only he could not hear, he shouted out over the rooftops:

"Sanctuary! Sanctuary!"

Far below, the crowd roared like the ocean.

CHAPTER TWELVE

❧ Sanctuary ❧

SANCTUARY, INDEED.

It's a sweet word, don't you think? I have heard that it comes from the the Latin word *sanctus*, which means sacred.

Here in Paris, Notre Dame is sacred. Our church is so sacred that no one has ever been turned away, no matter how great their crime. What is more, the law cannot pursue any person as long as he or she remains within the walls of the church.

Notre Dame has always been a refuge for people who have no place else to turn. This is a very old tradition in our city. Over the years, many people have sought sanctuary behind the thick stone walls of the cathedral.

Quasimodo knew this. He had known that if he and Esmeralda could reach the threshold of the church alive, they would receive its divine protection.

Now he and I sat together, high on the walls of our church, looking down at the girl as she lay on the stone floor beneath the bell towers. She breathed easily, I remember. I could tell she was alive, but lost in a deep swoon. The workmen had left behind a bundle of rags such as they use in cleaning up their patching work, and I watched as the hunchback arranged these into a rough bed and laid Esmeralda on it.

Then he sprang to the bell tower and leaped to the ropes, swinging the gigantic bells until their great copper tongues clanged joyously out over the city. It seemed that the whole cathedral thrummed with their sound.

I was happy, then. I had not heard the bells rung so well since the disastrous day in January when Quasimodo had ventured forth from our sanctuary.

Esmeralda heard the bells as well. I saw her open her eyes and sit up. She stared about her as if she expected to be in the land beyond death, as if the bells were heralding her entrance into the next world.

As soon as she regained consciousness, Quasimodo was kneeling at her side, his good eye glowing with joy. It must have frightened her to see him like that because she shrank back against the wall of the bell tower.

I saw from Quasimodo's face that he didn't wish to alarm her. He backed away. Then, as if thinking of something for the first time, he turned and dashed down the stone stairs. The girl rose and walked over to the edge of the roof, near where I perch.

For a moment I thought she might do something foolish. I thought she might hurl herself over the edge onto the pavement below. But she didn't. She simply stood and stared out in the direction of the Square de Grève.

She saw the gallows there, with two noosed ropes swinging uselessly in the breeze. She smiled then and absently placed a hand on my stone shoulder. Her hand felt small and tender, unlike the thick, heavy hand of the bell ringer.

Then, as the music of the bells slowed, I saw her turn. Quasimodo stood at the head of the stairway. In his arms was a woven willow basket containing two rounded loaves of bread, a cluster of fresh grapes, and a bottle of water. He placed these objects by her ragged bed, then backed off a few feet and watched. He made motions for eating and drinking.

Esmeralda hesitantly walked toward the basket and sat down beside it. Quasimodo nodded and pointed to his mouth. Esmeralda could wait no longer. Like a hungry animal, she took up the food, devouring every scrap.

That evening, the hunchback sat beside me and looked silently out over the city. The warmth of spring was coming, I could feel it in the air. Quasimodo laid a hand on my head and left it there for several moments before going down into the church, to his own quarters.

I understood. I understood that he had left Esmeralda in my care.

I kept a vigilant watch over the sleeping angel that night. But I did not need to be concerned. Whatever was happening in the streets below, I knew that up here, among the bells and the stars, there was no one on earth who would invade our sanctuary.

• • •

THE NEXT MORNING, WHEN ESMERALDA WOKE in the bell tower, Quasimodo was crouching faithfully beside her.

"Don't be afraid," I heard him say to her. His words were thick and clumsily formed, but they were so filled with kindness that I saw her smile, ever so faintly.

"Can you understand what I'm saying?" he asked.

"Yes," Esmeralda said quietly.

"I am deaf," he said with a sad smile, "so I cannot hear you. But if you will face me and speak slowly, I can read the words as they fall from your lips."

Esmeralda turned and, for the first time, made herself look full into the hunchback's face.

Quasimodo saw the horror of his twisted features reflected in the expression on the young girl's face.

"I know I am ugly to look upon," he admitted. "But you must understand—it has always been this way for me. It's horrible, isn't it? To be born into a body such as mine?"

Esmeralda gazed for a long, still moment into the hunchback's good eye. In a strange way, it seemed to me that her heart went out to him.

"You poor man," she whispered. "I have the odd feeling that you and I are linked in some way—as if our pasts are intertwined. But that's not possible, is it?"

"I don't see how," he said sadly.

Esmeralda asked, "Why did you risk so much to save me?"

Quasimodo smiled.

"I wanted to repay the kindness you showed me when I was tied to the wheel," he said simply. "You gave me water. . . . Do you remember?"

"Of course I remember."

"Why did you do that?" the hunchback asked.

"Because you were suffering, and there was no one else to help you. I cannot bear to see another being suffering. It reminds me of my goat, Djali.

"My poor goat, I wonder what has become of it? I found it one day with its leg caught in a wire fence. A bunch of boys were throwing rocks at it and calling it names. I drove the boys off and freed it. From that time forward, it became my companion. I do miss Djali."

Just then, as if thinking of something he had forgotten to do, Quasimodo rose and disappeared down the stairway. Several moments later, he came scrambling up the stairs with the kicking goat in his arms.

"Djali!" Esmeralda shouted. She took the white goat in her arms and rubbed it lovingly between the ears. Djali licked her face with its rough tongue.

"How did you find it?" she asked.

Quasimodo grinned through twisted teeth.

"Djali came to the doorway of the church this morning," he explained, "seeking sanctuary. I kept it tied in my chambers so that no one would disturb it. But I am so forgetful sometimes—I should have brought it to you earlier."

Esmeralda laughed.

"Oh, thank you—I'm sorry, how do you say your name?"

"Quasimodo."

"Yes, Quasimodo."

She rolled the word around on her tongue.

"It is a good name," she said. "The traveling people say that when you learn the name of someone, you begin to understand what lies beneath the surface."

They sat quietly then, neither saying anything, each lost in their own thoughts.

"In a strange way," Esmeralda said at last, "you and I are the same—we are both judged solely by the way we look. You are despised and I am admired—all because of an accident of birth. People look at me, and they see only the beauty of my face and the grace of my dancing feet. But they don't see how I suffer inside. They don't understand how lonely I am, with no mother or father and no family to call my own."

The bell ringer was gazing at her intently with his good eye. When he spoke, it was slowly, with great emotion.

"I understand," he said. "I am lonely as well. So few look beyond this ugly mask I wear. So few understand that my horrible, twisted body houses a human heart, the same as any other, with the same passions and longings."

"Yes," Esmeralda agreed. "We are the same, in that way."

She peered into his face.

"I see you, Quasimodo," she said softly. "I am seeing you for the first time. I see that you are good and kind and as lonely as I. I see that you are Quasimodo, my champion."

The hunchback glowed.

When he rang the morning bells, it seemed the shingles on the rooftops curled upward with joy. The April sunrise was burning over the hills, painting the skyline red.

CHAPTER THIRTEEN

❧ The Seeds of Rebellion ❧

MEANWHILE, IN THE WORLD BELOW US, ALL WAS not so safe and serene.

Frollo paced about his room. The rats say he was fairly foaming with rage.

"She still lives," he muttered to himself. "She lives and breathes, within these very walls! But I can't get at her. She might as well be hiding in the pyramids of Egypt! The hunchback is her protector now.

"If I try to venture up to the bell tower, he would tear me to pieces! I saw that wild look in his eye when he took her from the gallows. He has betrayed me! To think that I rescued him from death when he was a foundling on the church steps.

"I curse him! I curse the day I brought him into these walls! I will see that he is punished! But I cannot waste time with him now. First, I must find a way to quench this fire that rages in my breast."

Just then he heard a sound outside his window. Glancing out across the square of Notre Dame, he saw Pierre Gringoire setting up his juggling and fire-eating equipment on the bare cobblestones.

An idea flashed through the priest's brain, like a sudden stroke of lighting.

Opening the window, he called out, "You there, Master Gringoire. Come here, I want to talk with you!"

Pierre glanced up in surprise. He couldn't imagine why the priest would be calling him, but he set aside his equipment and walked to the window.

"I am only a poor man," Gringoire said, "I hope you do not mind that I perform my humble tricks outside the church here. It is such a well-traveled spot and the crowds here are very good—"

"Never mind all that," Frollo said; "I know who you are. I have seen you many times. But I have a matter I wish to discuss with you. Will you meet me at the side door in a few moments?"

The acrobatic poet bowed respectfully, "I am at your service, Father."

Frollo shut the window. As he walked rapidly down the corridor and out to the low-headed door facing the river, his plans fell into place with an astonishing clarity.

When he swung the door open, Gringoire was standing nervously on the paving stones.

"Come in," the priest said. Then he did his best to put the man at ease.

"Do you know who I am?" he asked.

Pierre nodded, "Of course, Dom Frollo."

The priest glanced up and down the corridor, then fixed Pierre with his burning eyes.

"I want to talk with you about something that is of great concern to us both," he began. "Isn't it true that you are married to the Gypsy girl they call Esmeralda?"

"In a manner of speaking, yes, but I have not seen her in some time. She was involved in a murder, you see—with which, I hasten to add, I had nothing to do— and when I last saw her she was on the gallows—"

"Yes," Frollo said impatiently, "I know all that. And if you have listened to the street gossip, you must know she now lives in Notre Dame, under the protection of the Church."

Gringoire nodded. "I have heard this."

"I am here to tell you that she is in great danger. Although the sanctuary of the Church is normally respected, I happen to know that the head magistrate of Paris has taken great offense that she was not hanged as he directed. He has obtained a decree from Parliament stating that the Church must give her up. She is to be executed in three days."

"What does this have to do with me?" Pierre asked.

"You are her husband, are you not?"

"I have never laid a hand on the girl. She married me to save me from being hanged, nothing more. She is beautiful, it is true, but not very affectionate. We have lived as brother and sister. I must confess, though, I do miss that clever goat she owned. The animal could do such artful tricks. If I had a goat like that—"

"I see," Frollo said. "I was hoping you might help me to save the girl."

"Why would you want to do that?"

Frollo spread his hands. "The Church must defend its authority; I'm sure you understand that."

"What would be in it for me?" Gringoire asked slyly.

"The Church has funds to help those who help us," Frollo said vaguely. "We could be quite generous."

Pierre's eyes shone.

"I am at your service," he said quickly. "What's the plan?"

Frollo gestured to the river. "Tonight I will steer a small boat down the Seine. We can bring Esmeralda out this door and slip her away downstream without anyone being the wiser."

The poet wrinkled his brow.

"That is a good plan," he said, "but why do you need me?"

Frollo leaned closer.

"I was a witness at Esmeralda's trial," the priest said. "Because of that, she does not trust me. She does not understand that I have everything to gain by seeing her free. If the girl is hanged, it will set a bad precedent for the Church. The sanctity of Notre Dame will be ruined if this kind of thing continues.

"But I cannot simply go to the bell tower and get her. If I could, I would. I need someone else, someone she knows and trusts. You, Master Gringoire, are that man. The Church depends upon you; what do you say?"

"It sounds very dangerous," Gringoire said, glancing at the purse that hung at Frollo's waist.

The priest smiled. He reached down and untied the leather bag of coins, placing it in Pierre's hand.

"This is just a small down payment," he murmured.

"I am your man," Gringoire declared. "What time shall we meet?"

"Be here at eight o'clock. I will be waiting with the boat."

Pierre bowed and, happily juggling the bag of coins, vanished down the alley.

EARLY THAT EVENING, SEATED AROUND A BANQUET table at an open-air tavern in the Court of Miracles, one of Pierre's ragged companions noticed the heavy purse hanging from his belt.

"You had a good day in the square of Notre Dame," he observed.

Pierre smiled. "A very good day," he said. He took a long drink from the tankard of wine that sat before him.

"I had no idea that street performing had become so profitable," the man said, "or have you finally branched out into picking pockets as well?"

Pierre shook his head. He had been drinking wine on an empty stomach for the last hour, and he was feeling light-headed and loose-tongued.

"No," he said, lowering his voice, "tonight I am being paid to undertake a dangerous mission."

"Really?" his drinking companion said. "Tell me more."

"Will you keep a secret?" Pierre asked.

"Of course."

"Well," he said, "if you must know, I am helping the priest to rescue Esmeralda from Notre Dame this evening."

Pierre thought he was speaking in a quiet voice. But at the mention of Esmeralda's name, several heads lifted from their drinks. One of them belonged to the beggar king, Clopin Trouillefou.

"What did you say?" the king asked.

Pierre's ragged companion stood and repeated Pierre's words in a loud voice.

Then he turned to the astonished poet and said, "You should know by now, my silly acrobatic friend, that there are no secrets in the Court of Miracles."

"Poor Esmeralda!" a woman sang out, "she has found sanctuary in the church, but it may as well be a prison."

"That's right," someone remarked.

"I am tired of having our people closed up in stone buildings," the king said to no one in particular.

"She's our sister," a peddler's wife said; "what can we do to save her?"

"We are an army," the king remarked. "We are a ragged army, one that smells of garlic and horse manure, that staggers with the legs of a drunkard, that has the ideals of a thief and the morals of a harlot, but, by the soul of the Holy Virgin, we are an army all the same!"

The circle of people around the table broke into spontaneous applause.

The king's wife leaned forward and placed a hand on his wine-stained sleeve.

"If you are going to make a speech, dear, you really should stand up."

"Very well," the king said drunkenly. With surprisingly little difficulty, he climbed up onto the table and drew his sword. Many heads turned in his direction.

"Hear me!" he bellowed. "We are an army, we are a ragged army, one that smells of—"

"You've already said that, dear," his wife said.

"All the same," the king retorted, "we must march on Notre Dame tonight. We will storm the cathedral and take Esmeralda back. I will not stand by and watch that lovely girl sealed away in the church like a wrinkled old nun!"

"Besides," a man shouted from the fireside, "Notre Dame is a treasure trove. The candlesticks, the wine cups, even the statues are made of silver and gold. And they sit there, day after day, gathering dust. Think what better use we would have for them!"

A roar of approval went up from the ragged mob.

"To arms!" the king shouted. "We will storm the cathedral and take back what is rightfully ours!"

As the mob worked itself into a frenzy, the dilapidated square became a beehive of activity. Barrels of weapons were rolled from the cellars and men began strapping on coats of tarnished armor. Children picked up handfuls of rocks; women fetched rags and jugs of kerosene and began making torches.

The entire square was electrified with the prospect of this great adventure.

Meanwhile, Pierre sat drunkenly at his table, watching the whirl of activity around him.

"Wait a minute," he said thickly, "no one has even asked me about my plan. . . ."

But no one was listening.

The Court of Miracles was preparing for war.

The ragged army would march with the rising of the moon.

CHAPTER FOURTEEN

❧ Storming the Cathedral ❧

THE MOON ROSE FULL AND BRIGHT OVER THE city, casting strange shadows across the familiar streets. The rats came scampering up the stone walls of Notre Dame, bringing me the news, their whiskers quivering in the cold light.

Before I saw the beggars' army approaching, I heard its footsteps.

Then I saw the torches bobbing about like fireflies in the square before our church. Despite the great number of people flooding into the square, they moved with very little chatter. They were, after all, an army of thieves, burglars, and cutthroats, people who knew the value of silence. But they were not silent for long.

In the cold expanse of the square, I heard the beggar king's great voice rising above the heads of the crowd, booming off the stone walls:

"To you, Deacon of Notre Dame," he shouted, "I, Clopin Trouillefou, King of the Court of Miracles and Bishop of Fools, proclaim the following: One of our sisters, falsely accused of witchcraft, has taken refuge in your church. As members of her tribe, we ask that she be returned to us immediately.

"Open your great doors and let her out. If you will

not surrender her to us, we will come and take her from you by force, along with whatever else we can lay our hands on. I plant my banner here on your doorstep as a testament to our determination. May God have mercy on you!"

As the mob cheered, the king stuck his banner into a flowerpot in front of the church. His brave act was illuminated by the shuddering flames of a thousand torches.

Of course, there was no response to Trouillefou's challenge. The bishop was not even here. He was far from Paris, visiting an abbey on the coast of southern France. None of the church officials answered in his behalf. Instead I am told that the priests and servants took one terrified look at the delegation on their doorstep and fled out the back door. Notre Dame stood empty and silent, guarded only by a deaf bell ringer and an army of stone statues.

No one answered the ruffian's challenge. Clopin motioned to a small knot of men armed with pincers, crowbars, hammers, and chisels. Without any further ceremony, they walked to the grand entrance of Notre Dame and began working at the doors with their tools. The clang of hammers and the scrape of metal drifted up from the street.

Lantern light appeared slowly in the windows of the buildings surrounding our square. A retired general in a white nightshirt leaned out from his balcony and shouted down at the mob.

"Go back to your hovels, you filthy heathens!" he ordered.

But the beggars' army was prepared. A dozen men shouldered their crossbows and fired. A barrage of metal-tipped arrows landed like a hailstorm around the balcony. Two of the swift shafts sank deep into the man's chest. He pitched forward and toppled over the railing, falling headfirst for more than a hundred feet before he struck the hard pavement. He lay crumpled on the stone street like an oversized rag doll that had been dropped from a great height.

After that, the windows swung closed.

Pausing from their noisy work at the doors, the men with the hammers swore in frustration.

"By the devil's hind leg," one man puffed, "this door is old and stiff in the joints!"

"The hinges are frozen with age," said his companion.

"They open each day for prayers," one man grumbled, "but why will they not open for us?"

"Stand back," a large man said sharply. He hefted a long-handled sledgehammer. With slow, measured strokes, he began to drive an iron spike into the lip between the doors. Sparks flew from his hammer; the spike sank deep into the metal, but still the great doors held.

"We will crack her!" Clopin shouted. "Keep on, boys, keep on! We will rescue Esmeralda even if it means tearing the doors from their hinges!"

"Think of the gold on the altar!" a woman shouted in encouragement.

"Think of the silver statues in the sanctuary!" said another.

"Think of the riches that will be ours!" shouted a third.

The crowd roared.

Just then, I felt a hand on my shoulder. I knew from its size and delicacy that it was the hand of Esmeralda. Roused from her sleep by the sounds of the mob, she leaned out over the edge of the roof, holding onto my shoulder for support. When she saw the army on our doorstep, with their gleaming torches and glittering weapons, her hand went to her mouth. Then, in a flash, she turned and was gone.

Had she rushed downstairs to join the members of her rowdy tribe? Had she run back to the safety of the bell towers? Or had she simply shrunk back into the shadows, paralyzed by fear?

A moment later, I had my answer. Close beside me, I heard the heavy breathing and felt the huge, lumbering presence of the hunchback.

Esmeralda pointed with a shaking finger at the crowd.

When Quasimodo looked down at the mob surging against the entrance to our church, he opened his lungs and howled like a demon. I saw the veins of his neck standing out like the stacks of a pipe organ.

But the vagabonds did not hear him. Their ears were filled with the shouts of their neighbors. They were so absorbed in the destruction of the doorway that they never thought to look above them.

Then I saw something I will never forget:

Quasimodo looked around wildly, sliding his good eye over the flat surface of the moonlit rooftop where we stood. At last, his glance fell on a huge oaken beam that the workmen had left behind. The squared timber was a foot thick and perhaps thirty feet long.

With the strength of a madman, Quasimodo worked his massive hands under one end. With a heart-rending grunt, he lifted it up, setting it on his shoulder. He dragged the beam across the stone walkway to the outer wall. There he set the timber down. The oaken log projected over the edge of the roof like the snout of a cannon.

Then he walked to the back of the timber and encircled it with his arms. Bending his great hunched back, the defender of Notre Dame pushed the beam forward. The heavy snout slid out over the edge of the roof, casting a strange moon shadow over the heads of the milling crowd below.

But no one looked up; no one saw what was coming. At last, when the great timber was hanging far over the edge, gravity took over. The massive beam tipped forward and began to fall.

"No!" I heard Esmeralda shout.

But it was too late.

The beam slid over the edge of the roof and fell in a long, slow arc, flipping end for end. When it crashed onto the pavement below, it sounded like a cannon shot.

There was no time to get out of the way. Dozens of people were crushed like insects.

The crowd surged back from the fallen beam like an ocean retreating at low tide. Then everyone was shouting at once. Not all of the unfortunates who lay under the beam were dead. The bloodcurdling shrieks of the wounded rose above the din. A pulverized mattress of quivering bodies lay on the stones. And in the pale light, I saw many flailing arms and legs protruding from underneath the squared timber. A lake of black blood was forming on the bottom steps of the church.

Esmeralda grabbed Quasimodo's arm.

"No," she shouted, "you must not do this!"

Quasimodo turned, his wild eye glaring, his disheveled hair drenched with sweat, his face twisted with rage.

"You look like a monster now!" the Gypsy girl cried. She must have known he couldn't hear her, but she shouted all the same. "I thought you were good and kind. But you are not! You are a beast!"

"I won't let them take you from me," he growled.

"You are not my champion," she said sharply; "you are just a horrible, twisted wreck of a man who kills without thinking! You are not like my Phoebus!"

But before Esmeralda could say more, Quasimodo bent down, picking up a squared block of building stone. With a furious grunt, he hurled it over the edge. The stone dropped swiftly, crushing two ragged women who were not fast enough to step aside.

"Look!" shouted a man holding a pickax. "Look up

on the roof! It's that horrible hunchback! May the devil take him!"

"Never mind the devil," the beggar king shouted. "We will do the job ourselves! Get that door open! I will tear him to pieces with my own hands!"

But the ragged soldiers of the beggars' army would not move. No man was brave enough to venture close to the great doors for fear he would be struck by a falling stone.

"By the snout of God!" Clopin shouted, "you're all a pack of fools! How can one misshapen man hold off an army of a thousand? Forward, men, forward!"

Roused by their leader's words, a dozen brave men—huddled under the small protection of a porch that spanned the entranceway—grabbed their tools and again set to work on the great doors.

Meanwhile, the men with crossbows shouldered their arms and fired on us. From where they stood, it was more than two hundred feet to the roof of our church, a very long shot for a crossbow. But they shot anyway. Most of the arrows fell short, breaking against the stone walls below us. Two or three struck the wall beside me. But the hunchback didn't retreat.

I have never seen him in such a fury. He used the building materials stacked on the roof as his weapons. Working like a demon, he hurled stones, wooden rafters, piles of rubbish, even workmen's tools, down on the surging crowd. The vagabonds scattered, pulling back from the doors of the church.

But the beggar king was not daunted. He swore he would crack the cathedral, even if it was the last thing he did. In a moment of sudden inspiration, his eyes fell on the massive beam that had caused so much agony and death just moments before.

"He has given us a battering ram!" The king was exultant.

Clopin's words gave the vagabonds new courage. They gripped the beam and crashed it furiously against the great doors. All of Notre Dame shook with the force of the blow. The doors groaned on their massive iron hinges. They groaned, but they held. A dozen times, the battering ram crashed into the doorway. But still the doors held.

The vagabonds panted like dogs and sweated like pigs. They strained their muscles, heaving the log with brutal force, shaking the church to its very foundations. After enduring the savagery of the blows for several moments, the aged wood of the door panels began to crack.

Through the cracks in the wood, the vagabonds could see the gleam of golden light. They knew that on the other side of the doors, six centuries of accumulated wealth lay waiting, ready to be plucked up and carried away by their dirty hands.

THE HUNCHBACK SENT AN AVALANCHE OF DEADLY objects pouring down on the soldiers of fortune. But the glow of gold was in their eyes now and there was no stopping them. As men were crushed by the fallen objects, others rushed forward to take their place. From where I hung, the battering ram looked like a many-legged monster, furiously ramming its head against the entrance to the cathedral. The doors were giving way.

But Quasimodo had not given up. Somewhere in the dark chambers of his skull, his thoughts spun with a furious clarity. He devised a new method to repel the attackers.

Out of the corner of my eye, I saw him use a torch to light a pile of wood scraps on the nearby walkway. A moment later he was throwing sheets of lead roofing material into the flames. I couldn't imagine what he was doing until I saw the sheets begin to melt and felt a scalding heat in the stones around me. Something was dripping down the walls of the church. Then I understood. The rain gutters were filling with molten lead.

At first, the lead sheets melted slowly. But as the fire roared, the lead began to flow like a stream, then a river, down the gutters and over the edge of the roof. The droplets fell slowly at first, then faster, in a steady, silvery stream. The jets of liquid lead spread out into a spray, pouring down onto the heads of the crowd.

The vagabonds scarcely had time to raise their hands before they were splattered about the head and shoulders. Some who were stung by the molten shower died on the spot. Others ran howling from the square, shaking their burning arms and legs.

The hunchback piled on sheet after sheet of the deadly metal. Soon the cobblestones of the square were puddled with the hissing, steaming liquid.

The attackers dropped their beam and retreated to the edge of the square.

Quasimodo stood high on the rampart walls. He thrust his fists into the air and howled down at them.

"Sanctuary!" he shouted. "Sanctuary!"

The fire crackled loudly behind him, sending a shower of sparks up into the sky. I saw that he was seized in a holy rapture. I knew then that he would have given his life gladly to save the Gypsy girl.

Esmeralda was not waiting to be saved. She was, after all, a girl who had learned to live by her wits. She must have known that now was the time to make her escape. In the confusion, she could easily slip away from the church and disappear into the crowded streets. She scooped Djali up in her arms and began feeling her way down the darkened stairway.

Quasimodo had taken the torch from the stairwell, and she had to grope along as best she could. She descended the cold stone steps, clutching Djali under her right arm, feeling her way along the stair wall with her left hand. She moved slowly, cautiously. One wrong move would send her tumbling down the steep stone steps.

Esmeralda was halfway between heaven and earth, with death waiting at either end.

CHAPTER FIFTEEN

❧ A Daring Escape ❧

Meanwhile, Pierre was drunkenly hobbling along the banks of the Seine, searching for the side door in the moonlight. At last he saw the low-headed entrance, set into the shadow of the stone wall. Nearby he noticed a small boat with a set of sturdy oars, rocking in the shallows of the river.

He was just about to knock when the door swung open. A tall figure, wrapped in a black cloak, said ominously, "May the devil strangle you, Gringoire, you are a half hour late!"

"I'm sorry, Dom Frollo," the poor man replied. "The streets were crowded and I lost track of the time and I . . ."

"Stop babbling, you fool," Frollo said, hauling him inside. "Are you ready?"

"Of course . . ."

The priest caught the heavy odor of the poet's breath in the darkness.

"You smell like a vineyard at harvest time!" he said sharply. "Can you climb?"

"Yes . . . as long as my legs will listen to my head," Gringoire said.

"I never should have trusted you, you idiot," Frollo

swore, "but it's too late now. I must go through with my plan. I will take you up the stairs. You will go the last flight yourself. Tell her that you were sent by her brave Captain Phoebus. That will fetch her along. She would follow her captain into the very depths of hell. Do you understand?"

"Yes, of course."

"Then come along quickly. Keep your hand to the right wall; that will guide you."

Climbing the stairs to the bell tower was no easy task. Pierre's head spun as he wound his way up one spiral staircase after another. As Frollo suggested, the poet-acrobat used his right hand to steady himself on the smooth stone wall.

After what seemed like a very long time, Frollo lit a fat yellow candle from his lantern.

"Take this," he said. "Go now. Go and bring me the girl."

As Pierre reached for the candle, Frollo grabbed him by the sleeve.

"Do not fail me," he said sternly.

Pierre nodded and stumbled ahead. The candle cast a weak light before him.

"By all the virgins of Paris," the poet swore, "this is the hardest fortune I've ever earned."

Pierre climbed the stone steps alone for several moments. Then, stopping to rest on a landing, he heard a sound above him. He strained his ears. Then he smiled. It was the bleating of a goat!

"Djali!" he whispered urgently. "Sweet Djali, I am coming for you!"

Just then Pierre saw the graceful feet of the Gypsy girl coming into view. A moment later, he saw the kicking form of the white goat in the flickering candlelight.

Esmeralda shielded her eyes with her hand. The goat bleated loudly.

"Who are you?" she asked.

"Don't you know me? I am your hero, your husband, Pierre! I should act offended," Gringoire teased. "Djali recognized me before you did!"

Esmeralda released the goat and watched as it scampered artfully down the stairs toward Gringoire.

"I thought for a moment you might be Captain Phoebus," Esmeralda said sadly.

Pierre scratched the goat between the ears.

"Ah, yes, Phoebus," he said slyly; "he sent me to fetch you. He has a boat waiting on the river just outside the church. Don't worry, Esmeralda, he has not forgotten you!"

The girl's face brightened in the candlelight.

"Really?"

"Really," Pierre said, improvising as he went. "He told me that he would give his life a thousand times to free you!"

"Then why didn't he come himself?" she asked.

Pierre shook his head. "He is putting down a rebellion at the moment. But he sent me to fetch you. He will meet us later. Come along now," he said and reached out for Esmeralda's hand.

Still hesitating, the girl asked: "You will take me to Phoebus, you promise?"

Pierre put his hand over his heart.

"On my honor as your husband, I promise."

He may have even believed it himself.

Esmeralda slipped her cold and trembling hand into Pierre's and they descended the slippery stone stairs. When they reached the landing where Frollo stood with his cloak pulled across his face and his lantern held low to the floor, Esmeralda drew back.

"Who is he?" she asked.

"A friend, sent by Phoebus to assure your escape," Pierre lied.

Esmeralda shivered.

"Come along," the poet said. He pushed the goat along before him.

"Why is your friend so quiet?" Esmeralda asked.

"Because his parents were talkative people and he grew sick of chatter," Pierre said. "But Esmeralda, we must not talk now, we are almost outside."

They were indeed almost outside. As Frollo led the way, they slipped down the darkened corridor and through the side door. They quickly climbed into the boat. Esmeralda sat in the bow, searching the shoreline for her Phoebus. Pierre sat in the stern, cradling Djali on his lap. Frollo sat between them, close by the oars. He drew a long knife and cut the rope. The current pulled the boat away from shore. Frollo swung the oars out from their locks, dipping them into the cold-running river.

QUASIMODO RAN FRANTICALLY BACK AND FORTH on the walkway. The fire roared at his back; the molten lead hissed over the edge of the roof. Far below, the attackers had abandoned their battering ram.

But they had not given up. Instead, they brought ladders and ropes and were scrambling up the facade of the church, climbing like living gargoyles up the outer walls. Caught by the spray, some burned and fell. But some held on. They clung to the stonework and made their way slowly up the wall, resting on the narrow ledges, then climbing higher.

One enterprising burglar put his booted foot through a window, shattering the stained glass. Another enlarged the hole by beating at it with a wood ax. Soon a steady stream of dark bodies was crawling in through the broken window and dropping down into the cathedral. Moments later, I saw the great doors of the church swing open from the inside. A grasping, clutching flood of humanity, all teeth and fingers and glittering eyes, rushed into the quiet chambers of Notre Dame.

Some of the men, I suppose, were bent on simple thievery. Some were determined to rescue Esmeralda. And some, a bloodthirsty few, were bent on taking revenge against the hunchback, who had killed so many of their companions during the furious battle.

But none of these things happened. On the edge of the square, a man came riding, with a drawn sword and glistening armor, backed by a legion of the king's cavalry. The disturbance in the square had awakened the neighborhood, and frightened citizens had sent word to the night watch. Phoebus had taken command of a detachment of the king's best horsemen. Now he rode into the mob, determined to put down the rebellion.

The fight was furious. The beggars' army far outnumbered the riders. It seemed at first that the vagabonds might win. They pulled the soldiers from their horses and beat them with their crude weapons. Women, children, even wild dogs set upon the fallen riders. I saw the animals' claws and teeth flashing in the torchlight.

But the beggars were on foot and poorly armed. They were hemmed in on all sides and had no way to retreat from the slashing swords and thrusting lances of the king's men. The cavalry swept the square like a windstorm, leaving a wake of broken bodies behind.

Phoebus and his men were soon clambering on horseback up the stone steps of the church. A few thieves, but only a few, had rushed from the cathedral, their arms stacked with loot. Phoebus's men were easily able to overtake them and cut them down.

Now, in the apartments overlooking the square, the frightened citizens gathered their courage.

Directing murderous fire from above, they began aiming their household weapons at the vagabonds.

I saw it all by torchlight. I saw the stamping horses and the stumbling, fleeing beggars. I heard the singing steel of sword blades and the desperate curses of fighting and dying men. The smell of burning flesh rose to my open nostrils. I could not close my eyes against it. I had no choice. I had to look. I had to witness each ignoble death and record each scream and curse in my memory of stone. It was the first battle I had ever seen so close at hand. And I was horrified by it.

Quasimodo was not horrified. He was joyful. When he saw the vagabonds repulsed from the church, he knelt on the edge of the roof and raised his arms to heaven. He howled the howl of the victorious.

He was so filled with the heat and joy of the battle that he didn't see what I saw: He didn't see the single, sharp-tipped arrow, arching high through the air and falling fast toward the spot where he knelt.

CHAPTER SIXTEEN

❧ Lost and Found, ❧ Found and Lost

THE ARROW SANK DEEP INTO THE MEAT OF THE bell ringer's right thigh. At first he didn't seem to notice. Then I saw him bend his great head and look at the feathered shaft protruding from his leg as a bull might look at a fly that had landed on his rump.

Twisting his mouth, Quasimodo grasped the shaft with both hands and tried to yank the arrow out. But the metal tip was driven deep and all he managed to do was enlarge the hole.

Then I saw the blood welling out of the wound, soaking the rough cloth of his pants and puddling on the stone beneath him.

But Quasimodo had seen a great deal of blood that night, and I suppose that a little more didn't matter much to him, even if it was his own.

The hunchback rose and hobbled to the bell towers. He searched wildly for a few moments, then slumped against the wall of the tower. Only then did he realize that Esmeralda was gone.

ESMERALDA SHIVERED IN THE BOW OF THE SMALL boat. The pigeons, fluttering about the rooftops, saw her clearly, swooping low to hear what she said.

"Where are we going?" she asked Pierre.

"To meet Phoebus," he reminded her.

"But where is he now?"

The poet pointed to the torchlight in the square of Notre Dame. They could see glimpses of the square from the river. The scattered sounds of battle still rang from the rooftops.

"There is an awful fight going on there," Gringoire said. "I'm glad I'm not part of it."

"What's it all about?" she asked.

"Why, Esmeralda, don't you understand? The entire Court of Miracles turned out tonight to storm the cathedral and free you!"

But before the Gypsy girl could say more, the boat bumped against the shore. The man in black stowed his oars and, half crouching, tied the boat to an old post driven into the riverbank.

"Well," Pierre said, trying to sound cheerful, "this must be where we disembark."

With the goat in his arms, he hopped ashore and disappeared into the darkness.

Esmeralda stared down at the rippling water. It was cold and black, and the sound of it filled her ears, blotting out everything. When she looked up, she saw the stranger in black standing on the shore, reaching out for her. His fingers closed around her wrist. He pulled her from the boat and up onto dry land.

Esmeralda looked around.

"Pierre!" she called, "which way do we go? Djali?"

There was no answer.

The tall man began pulling her along then, walking rapidly up the riverbank and onto the streets. He said nothing. But he held the girl's wrist so tightly that she had to clench her teeth in pain.

At last, they were standing on the edge of a large, moonlit square. Esmeralda recognized it—it was the Square de Grève. The gallows stood tall and ghostly in the moonlight.

"Do you know where you are?" the man said, speaking so low she could hardly hear him.

Esmeralda tried to pull her hand back. As she did, the man struggled to hold her. The high collar of his cloak fell back, revealing his thin face and tortured eyes. His face was like a death mask, waxy and cold, in the moonlight.

"I knew it was you!" Esmeralda said. "I was hoping I was wrong. I was hoping that Pierre was telling me the truth and that Phoebus really had sent you to save me. But now I see—"

"What you see," the priest whispered, "is a man tormented by your beauty. I must have you—or no man will have you. Your life is in my hands—and my soul is in yours."

"Go away!"

"Don't say that. Don't say that until you hear what I have to offer. I am the only one who can save you.

The army of ruffians who came to rescue you is in shambles. Your husband seems to prefer the company of your white goat. And as for your brave Captain Phoebus, he and his soldiers have strict orders to turn you over to the hangman as soon as you set foot outside Notre Dame."

"You're lying."

"No, I am not. The soldiers are just a block away. I can go get them now. They would hang you within the hour. Or you can go away with me. I have everything arranged. I will take you downriver in the boat. I have money. I am prepared to give up my place in the church. We can go to another land. We can live there together. You will dance for me; I will make you happy—"

"Never!"

The priest shook her with a violence that almost snapped her wristbones.

"You must choose—between me and the gallows!" he shouted.

"Then I choose death," Esmeralda said.

"Is that your final answer?" Frollo asked.

"Yes."

The priest's face turned ashen and stony. He encircled her throat with his long fingers.

Just then there was a shout, the high shriek of an old woman, from across the square.

The priest turned to see a movement in the barred window at the base of Roland Tower.

"Sister Gudule!" he shouted, "here is your Gypsy girl! She is about to die!"

"Death to her!" the old woman shouted. "Death to her and her godless race!"

"You may take your vengeance," the priest shouted, pulling Esmeralda across the square toward the recluse's window.

Before Esmeralda knew what was happening, Frollo had dragged her to the window of the old woman. He took the rope belt from his cassock and tied the girl's thin wrists to the iron bars.

A withered, whitened arm reached out from the window and grabbed Esmeralda by the hair.

"That's it!" the priest shouted. "Hold her tight, old woman! I will go and fetch the king's guards. I hear men on horses, right over there. You will see her hanged!"

Sister Gudule threw back her head and laughed. Her weird laughter echoed off the cold stones of the tower.

Frollo rushed away, his eyes fiery with hatred and pain.

The old woman shook Esmeralda's head; her cold fingers dug deep into the roots of the girl's hair. The Gypsy girl tried to pull free, but the old woman held her with a grip of iron.

"They are going to hang you," Sister Gudule taunted.

Esmeralda twisted her head so that she was facing the window.

"What have I ever done to you?" she asked tearfully.

"What have you done to me?" the old woman repeated, her voice dripping with hatred and anger. "Listen and I'll tell you: I once had a child, a beautiful baby girl. If she were still alive, she would be about your age. But she is dead now! The Gypsies stole her from me! They stole her and left a horrible monster in her place! Your Gypsy mothers did this!"

"My mother was not a Gypsy!" Esmeralda shouted. "She was a Frenchwoman, from Reims! I was taken from her when I was small!"

"Lies!" Sister Gudule shouted. "This is all a Gypsy lie! I myself was from Reims, I should know! I should know how I lost my daughter! I have thought about it every day for the last fifteen years. Look here," Sister Gudule released the girl's hair long enough to reach down into her cell.

"Look here," the old woman was saying, "look at this tiny shoe. This was hers. This is all I have left of my dear sweet Agnes!"

Esmeralda strained her eyes in the moonlight.

"Wait a moment," she said, "let me see that shoe!"

The old woman held up the shoe. A glimmer of hope came into her voice. "Do you know something?" she asked. "Do you know something about my daughter?"

Esmeralda tried to draw the cloth bag from her neck, but her hands were tied to the bars and her fingers could not reach down into the folds of her dress. Over her shoulder, she heard the sound of horses in the street leading to the square.

"Help me!" Esmeralda shouted, "I am your daughter!"

"What?"

"Yes! You are my mother! I can prove it! Draw the bag from my neck, look for yourself."

The old woman leaned far out the window, drew out the cloth bag, and found the matching shoe.

"Agnes?" Sister Gudule said, tears welling up in her eyes. "Can it really be you? My dear sweet Agnes, come back to me after all these years?"

The old woman reached through the bars, smoothing back the tangled, rumpled hair that she had pulled with such violence just a few moments before.

"Mother," Esmeralda said, "help me! Will you help me? They are coming to hang me!"

The old woman's bony fingers worked at the rope holding Esmeralda's hands.

Meanwhile, the sound of horses' hooves was echoing like a death knell on the abandoned streets, just outside the square.

"Quickly," Esmeralda breathed, "they are coming for me!"

Sister Gudule slipped the girl's hands from the rope and swung the iron grate open, pulling her into the tower just as two horsemen wheeled into the square.

"Hide in the shadows," the old woman said sharply. Then, to herself, she muttered, "God would not do this to me. He would not take my daughter from me now, now that I have found her after all these years of suffering and pain!"

Just then, there was the sound of voices outside the window of Roland Tower.

"Old woman," Esmeralda heard the voice of the sergeant of the watch, "we are looking for a Gypsy witch who has escaped from Notre Dame. The archdeacon himself sent me. He said he left her tied to your window."

"I don't know what you are speaking of," Sister Gudule said. "I was sleeping."

"Listen," the soldier said sternly, "don't lie to me. The entire area is in the midst of a rebellion. You can't tell me you slept through all that. She was tied right here to the window. Look on the ground, here is the rope from his cassock."

"Yes," the old woman said, "that's right. She was tied. But she freed herself and she ran away."

"Which direction?"

The old woman pointed a bony finger toward Notre Dame.

"What? She ran in the direction of the battle? Old woman, you are lying to me! I have half a mind to let the Gypsy girl go and hang you instead!"

Scarcely breathing, Esmeralda huddled in the shadows.

"I won't rest until the Gypsy girl is hung!" the sergeant vowed. Then he turned to his companion.

"Captain Phoebus," he said, "give me a detachment of your men and I will scour the neighborhood."

"They are yours," the captain replied. Then he

swung onto his horse. "I must get back to my men," he shouted, then spurred his horse.

When Esmeralda heard her hero's voice, she pushed past her mother and sprang to the window.

"Phoebus!" she shouted after him. "I am here!"

But Phoebus was gone.

"No," Sister Gudule said, pulling Esmeralda from the window. But it was too late.

The sergeant of the guard threw his head back and laughed.

"Two mice in one trap, eh?" He blew his whistle.

A moment later, a half-dozen men came galloping into the square. They dismounted and tied their horses to an iron ring set into the outside wall of Roland Tower.

The sergeant slapped his leg with his riding gloves. "I will likely get a promotion for this," he said to himself.

"Fetch me the hangman," he said. One of the soldiers mounted and rode off at a full gallop.

The sergeant motioned to the window. "Bring me the young one," he said.

But when one of the guards pulled the grate aside and reached into the darkness of the tower, the old woman sank her twisted teeth into the soldier's hand.

He howled like a demon and jerked his bloodied hand back as if it had been bitten by a mad dog.

"Kill the old one if you have to," the sergeant said coldly, "but bring me the girl."

The men in armor hesitated.

The leader turned in disbelief to his men. "What kind of men are you, afraid of an old woman?"

"Go ahead," Sister Gudule shrieked, "go ahead, brave Sergeant, stick your head through this window. I will tear your eyes out with my own nails!"

The soldier spat on the pavement. "Tear down the wall," he ordered.

A moment later the soldiers were working at the crumbling stone of the tower with their lances and pickaxes. The stones fell away easily. Inside they heard the old woman snarling like a hungry tigress defending her young.

Drawing their swords, the soldiers pushed their way through the opening.

Just then, a man with a hangman's noose coiled over his shoulder appeared at the sergeant's side.

"Do you have her?" he asked.

The sergeant nodded.

In the darkness of the tower, they could hear the sounds of a ferocious struggle, the clang of steel against the tower walls, and the unearthly shrieking of the old hag.

In a moment, it was over. The panting soldiers carried Esmeralda kicking into the moonlight. Close behind her, blood streaming from her forehead, was the old woman, crawling on hands and knees from the rubble of the tower.

The hangman bound Esmeralda's hands behind her and threw her over his shoulder like a sack of wheat. He was a massive man, with broad shoulders and a slow, somber look on his face.

"Please," Esmeralda begged, "you can't hang me now. I have just found my mother, my true mother. We have been separated all these years. It's too cruel to think that you would hang me. Before I had nothing to live for. But, now, I am no longer an orphan. Don't you understand?"

When the hangman said nothing, she wailed, "I don't want to die! Can't you see that? I am alive now and I want to stay alive!"

"You shall die," a voice said.

Someone was walking beside them now. It was the priest, Dom Frollo.

They were at the scaffold. The first rays of dawn were breaking across the sky. I could see the whole pitiful scene from the roof of Notre Dame. I saw the hangman slip the noose around the poor girl's neck. I saw the priest standing on the platform. I saw him throw back his head and laugh.

The square before the church was quiet. The laughter of the priest carried a long way, across the bleeding and broken bodies that littered the square, across the rubble of the battle, and up to my pointed ears.

With a sudden, powerful motion, the hangman pulled the rope tight and Esmeralda swung out above the cobblestones, her dancing feet thrashing in the air.

CHAPTER SEVENTEEN

❧ Four Tragedies ❧

IN HER LAST MOMENTS, THE GYPSY GIRL KICKED her small feet, as if she was reaching out for the earth far below. But the hangman had done his work well. She struggled for a few moments, but only a few. Her delicate neck twisted. Then she went limp, swaying gently in the morning light, like a colorful flag, hung out on festival days.

I saw the hangman turn to Frollo and shout and point behind him. But it was too late. A dark, shambling form climbed the wooden stairs and rose up behind the priest, seizing him under the arms.

Even in the slanting morning light, I could tell it was Quasimodo. I watched, helpless, as the hunchback snatched Frollo from his feet, lifted him high into the air, and hurled him down onto the cobblestones. It was a short fall, only twenty feet. But the priest fell headfirst, snapping the bones of his neck.

At the sight of the raging beast who had climbed onto the scaffold with him, the hangman had dropped the rope and leaped down off the platform, scurrying away toward the soldiers who had gathered to watch the Gypsy girl hang.

When the hangman released the rope, Esmeralda's

body fell and landed on the rough boards of the scaffold. Now Quasimodo sprang to her and knelt, cradling her head in his heavy hands, bending his face low to hers, as if he could blow the breath of life back into her. But even I could see that it was no use. I could tell from the way her head jutted from her shoulders that she was dead.

The soldiers did not move on the hunchback as I thought they would. They did not lift their weapons against him. Instead, they stood in an astonished circle around the gallows and watched the life slowly bleed out of him. The arrow still protruded from his thigh and he had left a winding trail of blood on the cobblestones of the Square de Grève. I understand there is a large artery in the human leg that, once severed, will drain away the lifeblood in a very short time.

I do not know what happened to the bodies of the dead. I suppose the cold forms of Esmeralda and Quasimodo and Claude Frollo were thrown into the river, along with the other corpses that were hauled away that morning. I suppose their bones and flesh mingled with all the others who had died that night: soldiers, priests, and beggars sank together into the Seine. They would be carried away downstream, to the saltwater of the ocean, where they would become food for fish.

I KNOW A FEW THINGS ABOUT THE ONES WHO SURVIVED the night.

I know that Pierre Gringoire managed to save both the goat and his own skin. I know he lived for a very long time and went on to become a great writer of tragedies.

I know that Captain Phoebus, who never dreamed how much hardship he had caused, came to his own tragic end: he was married and spent the remainder of his days attending dinner parties and dances.

As for the members of the Court of Miracles, they simply went back to their dismal lives. They had not gained any treasures during their ill-fated siege against the church. But they had learned that the king of France—or his soldiers—certainly knew how to deal with a mob.

Around the greasy campfires in the Court of Miracles, many stories were told about the hunchback and Esmeralda. Some said their ghosts continued to haunt Notre Dame and that on moonlit nights you could see them walking, side by side, on the cold stone walkway between the bell towers. But you must remember, these are a superstitious, ignorant people. They are like children, making up stories to explain the things they cannot understand.

But still, even after all these years, I will confess that I sometimes see things on moonlit nights— nothing distinct, you understand—just the palest suggestion of a dancing form, passing among our towers. And sometimes, when the wind blows cold and wet from the east, I imagine that I feel the comforting, heavy hand of Quasimodo on my shoulder and the warm touch of his misshapen cheek against my own.

Of all the humans I have seen, he was by far the noblest and the one who taught me the most. I now realize that because of Quasimodo, I am almost human.

❦ About Victor Hugo ❦

THE HUNCHBACK OF NOTRE DAME WAS WRITTEN by a man who started out much the same as Pierre Gringoire: writing tragedies, plays, and poetry for the people of France.

Victor Hugo was born in 1802. Because his father was a general in Napoléon's army, the family traveled a great deal while Hugo was still very young. He lived in Italy and Spain before beginning his education in Paris. All in all, Hugo had only three years of formal schooling.

As a young man, Hugo lived in an attic in Paris and devoted himself to his writing. His first volume of poetry was published in 1822. He became interested in the romantic movement in France, which sought to break down old traditions and replace them with more liberated forms of expression.

The struggle of the common people against an oppressive government is a recurrent theme in Hugo's work. *The Hunchback of Notre Dame*, which was published in 1831, painted the lot of the common people in broad, dramatic strokes, in a compelling language that no one could ignore.

Fired by his success in literature, Hugo turned to politics. He was elected to the French Parliament in

1845. When Louis-Napoléon became emperor of France in 1851, Hugo opposed him and was forced to leave the country for nineteen years. Hugo lived in exile on the island of Guernsey. It was there that he wrote his most famous novel, *Les Misérables*.

After the fall of the emperor in 1870, Hugo returned to France, becoming an active member of the newly formed Senate. At home in his beloved Paris, he continued to work for political change and wrote with a passionate intensity until his death in 1885.